The Listener

Tove Jansson

Sort Of
BOOKS
www.sortof.co.uk

The Listener

Tove Jansson

Translated from the Swedish by
Thomas Teal

The Listener © Tove Jansson 1971; first published as *Lyssnerskan*
  by Schildts Förlags Ab, Finland.
English translation © Thomas Teal and Sort Of Books 2014
All rights reserved
Thanks to Sophia Jansson for her encouragement and advice.

No part of this book may be reproduced in any form without permission
from the publisher except for the quotation of brief passages in reviews.
This English translation first published in 2014 by
Sort Of Books, PO Box 18678, London NW3 2FL.

Typeset in Goudy and Gill Sans to a design by Henry Iles.
Printed in Italy by Legoprint.

>   Sort of Books gratefully acknowledges the financial
>   assistance of FILI – Finnish Literature Exchange

FILI

160pp.
A catalogue record for this book is available from the British
Library

ISBN 978-1908745361

To my brother, Per Olov

Tove Jansson's artwork for the original Swedish publication of
Lyssnerskan (*The Listener*), Bonniers, 1971.

Contents

The Listener...........................9
Unloading Sand........................21
The Birthday Party....................26
The Sleeping Man......................32
Black-White...........................40
Letters to an Idol....................52
A Love Story..........................62
The Other.............................70
In Spring.............................78
The Silent Room.......................81
The Storm.............................85
Grey Duchesse.........................90
Proposal for a Preface................95
The Wolf..............................98
The Rain.............................110
Blasting.............................115
Lucio's Friends......................125
The Squirrel.........................133

The Listener

AUNT GERDA WAS FIFTY-FIVE when it began, and the first sign of change was in her letters. They grew impersonal.

She was a quiet, well-to-do woman of ordinary appearance. Nothing about her was provocative, disturbing, or exaggerated. But she was a good letter writer. Not brilliant, of course, not amusing, but in her letters Aunt Gerda took up and examined every detail communicated to her without ever subjecting her correspondents to meddlesome advice. They had grown accustomed to the fact that she replied at once, not anxiously but with care and serious interest. Her letters often ended with a wish for a productive autumn or a pleasant spring, and this generous time limit seemed to give them full freedom to take their time with their next letter.

Reading one of Aunt Gerda's letters was exciting, like reliving one's own experiences, only this time dramatised and clarified on a wider stage, with a Greek chorus observing and underlining the action. And with the certain assurance that she would never reveal the confidences with which she was so often rewarded.

Now, and for some time past, Aunt Gerda waited weeks and months with her replies, and when she finally did write, her letters were marred by unworthy excuses, her handwriting had grown large and loose, and she wrote on only side of the paper. And her masterfully detailed sympathy had lost its warmth.

When a person loses what might be called her essence – the expression of her most beautiful quality – it sometimes happens that the alteration widens and deepens and with frightening speed overwhelms her entire personality. This is what happened to Aunt Gerda. Soon she was dropping names, forgetting birthdays, faces, promises. She began coming late – the woman who always used to sit and wait on the steps and still be the first to arrive. Her tardy presents were too expensive, too big, too impersonal, and accompanied by embarrassing excuses. No longer the lovingly calculated gifts that she had made herself. No longer the pretty, touching Christmas cards put together from pressed flowers, angels, and occasional glitter. Now she bought expensive, glossy cards with printed wishes for joy and happiness.

As a result, the dispatches Aunt Gerda sent out bore sad witness to her transformation – a vast, depressing lack of attentiveness. People carry their loved ones with them. They are forever present, and life is full of easily grasped opportunities to show them one's affection. It costs so little and achieves so much. Her siblings and nieces and nephews and friends all felt that Gerda had lost her style, her sense of responsibility, that she had grown self-centred from living alone – or perhaps it was the inescapable forgetfulness that comes with age. But deep down they knew that the change was deeper. It was inexplicable and basic and a matter of shifts in the mysterious stratum that forms a person's character and worth.

Aunt Gerda was aware of what was happening to her, but she didn't understand it. The acts and attitudes that had been a voluntary adaptation and concession to her own kindheartedness became very suddenly an overwhelming burden. She was plagued by self-reproach. Time, the passing hours, the need to be punctual, was perhaps the most difficult of all. Days with an afternoon or evening invitation had their own timing, capricious and anxious even in the morning. In an odd way, they were bifurcated, so to speak. On the one side was Aunt Gerda's genuine anticipation as she arranged the things she wanted to have with her when she left home. And on the other side was a great uncertainty with regard to names, faces, words, and the grasp of detail and context that must be complete for anyone who loves.

On that side, too, was the enemy – time. Time that relentlessly approaches a certain predetermined second at which someone on the other side of a door begins to wait. A second is less than one breath, and everything that follows is too late, more and more too late. When Aunt Gerda approached the appointed time for departure, her unease became unbearable. She made peculiar mistakes, misread the clock, started doing small irrelevant chores. She grew suddenly tired and fell asleep in her chair, and if she'd set the alarm clock, she might go out on the stairs or into the attic for no reason at all just when it rang. When the poor woman finally managed to arrive – too late – she couldn't keep herself from annoying her host and hostess with desperate and overly detailed excuses.

Time passed and things did not improve. It is difficult when a person one values behaves badly, so much so that no one can rush in and help. In the middle of a sentence, Aunt Gerda would forget whether one of her sister's children was a boy or a girl and stop abruptly in a panic and then say, very softly, "I mean, how is your ... child?" She introduced herself to people she'd known for years, and her fear was so visible that it cast gloom on everyone she knew.

It is important to describe all this in order to understand Aunt Gerda's behaviour in the late winter of 1970.

Probably few of us pay adequate attention to all the things constantly happening to the people we love, a steady, compact mass of activity that can be grasped in its entirety only by a person like Aunt Gerda – before she changed, of course. Loved ones take exams and degrees or fail to take them; they get pay rises and grants or fail to get them; they have children and miscarriages and neuroses; they have trouble with the help and their sex lives and teenage rebelliousness and misconceptions and money and maybe their stomachs or their teeth; they lose their faith or their jobs or their self-confidence or the person they're trying to live with and then lose themselves in politics or self-deception or disappointment or ambition; they get disloyalty and funerals and all sorts of frights thrown right in their faces; and eventually they get wrinkles and a thousand other things they hadn't expected – and I had all of that in the palm of my hand, thought Aunt Gerda in distress. It was all as clear as an etching and I made no mistakes! I never made a mistake. What is it that's happened to me?

She often woke at night and was unable to fall back to sleep. Sometimes she wondered where the calm, happy people might be found, if such people even existed, and whether she might dare to let herself be captivated if she ever did find them. No, Aunt Gerda thought. They too carry some secret weight, they too hide some burden that they want to share.

Letters, gifts, and affection's glossy greetings are important. But the ability to listen face to face is even more important, a great and rare art. Aunt Gerda had always been a good listener, aided perhaps by her difficulty in expressing herself and by her lack of curiosity. She had been listening to friends and relatives ever since she was young, listening while they talked about themselves and each other, carrying them with her in a huge, artfully constructed mental map of crisscrossing lives. She listened with her whole large, flat face, unmoving, leaning slightly forward, with downcast eyes, though she would occasionally look up, quickly and in obvious distress. She didn't touch her coffee and let her cigarette burn down. Only in the short pauses that even a tragic tale leaves open for trivial but necessary explanations did she permit herself a lungful of smoke and a deep swallow of coffee before replacing the cup on its saucer carefully and without a sound. In essence, Aunt Gerda was not much more than silence. Afterwards, it was difficult to reconstruct what she had said, maybe only a breathless questioning – Yes? Really? – or a quick expression of sympathy.

As the years went by, and Aunt Gerda's weight of insight grew, it troubled no one that she knew so much about them. They counted on her protective faculty; they let themselves be misled by her peculiar air of innocence and neutrality. It was like telling secrets to a tree or a devoted pet and never having afterwards that queasy feeling that you've given yourself away. But now it was as if Aunt Gerda had lost her innocence. Her broad face listened the same way – open, unfurrowed – and, though her brief expostulations were the same, they had lost something of their shyness and the simple desire to know in order to understand and so to love. There was not the same pain in her eyes, and she had developed an annoying, involuntary gesture that was, perhaps, apologetic.

Not many of them called Aunt Gerda that winter and spring. Her apartment grew very quiet and peaceful, she listened only to the elevator or sometimes to the rain. She often sat at her window and watched the change of seasons. She had a bay window in a semicircular projection that was rather chilly. The window was round and now in March embellished with icicles. The spikes of ice were thick and finely chiselled by running water. In the evening, they turned blue. No one called and no one came. It seemed to her the window was a great eye looking out over the city and the harbour and a strip of the gulf under ice. The new silence and emptiness was not entirely a loss; it was something of a relief. Aunt Gerda felt like a balloon, untied, soaring off its own way. But, she thought, it's a balloon that's bouncing against the ceiling and can't get free.

She understood that this was no way to live; human beings are not built to float. She needed an earthly anchor of meaning and care so she didn't get lost in confusion. One day, with water dripping from the eaves, Aunt Gerda decided to exercise her memory and pull herself back to the simple plane where her life had its justification. She made a list of the devoted people she could remember and of their children and grandchildren and other relatives, and made an earnest effort to remember when they were all born. The paper was much too small. Aunt Gerda rolled out a long piece of shelf paper on the dining room table and held it down with drawing pins. She made a big black dot, a round head for each of them, with the name and birth date and title in a pretty little oval. She placed their children alongside, connected to their parents with a red line. She put all romantic relationships in pink – double lines for unconventional or forbidden alliances. Aunt Gerda became engrossed. Some heads were burdened with perfect coronas of pink – like galactic suns, impressive and probably regrettable.

For the first time, Aunt Gerda became aware of her own private commentary, which was not entirely benign. She bought crayons in new colours and worked on conscientiously – divorces in violet, hate in crimson, loyalty lines in bright cerulean. The dead were grey. She left space for memory to provide all the facts and data that fill and surround a life. She had time now to remember. Time was no longer a danger; it moved in parallel with herself and later on she would nail it down in a neat little oval. Aunt Gerda noted thefts of money, of children, of work and love and trust. She remembered those who drowned one another in bad conscience or who froze each other out. She drew their lines and erased them to make them more precise. Time was no longer bifurcated, and she listened only to her inner voice. Her memory delivered up tones of voice and silences, faces that clenched and went naked and then closed again, and all the mouths that talked and talked. Aunt Gerda gathered them all and put them to good use. What she wrote in the ovals lost its weight and its pain but retained its meaning. Aunt Gerda's memory opened like a great seashell; every twist was clear and exact and retained its echo. Even very distant echoes came gradually closer, like whispers.

As the spring wore on, Aunt Gerda transferred her great life map onto better, thicker paper. She was bothered a little by repetitions that might strike some as banal, but all human behaviour follows quite primitive rules. And anyway she did have one unique event – an attempted murder. She inscribed it in purple and felt a little cold thrill, maybe not unlike the thrill a stamp collector feels when he fastens a priceless misprint into his collection.

Sometimes Aunt Gerda sat quietly without trying to remember, simply immersed in her solar system of past and emerging lives, sensing the future changes in the lines and ovals, inevitable in the light of obvious cause and effect. She felt a desire to forestall what must happen, to draw her own lines, new lines, maybe in silver and gold, since all the other colours were taken. She toyed recklessly with the idea of making the dots and ovals movable, game pieces that could shift their context and create new constellations and entanglements.

Now and then the telephone rang, but Aunt Gerda said she had a cold and couldn't see anyone.

Towards the end of April, Aunt Gerda began to draw a frame around her map, a frame of small, peculiar ornaments, not unlike the distracted figures a person doodles in a telephone catalogue while listening. She was listening, inwardly, to words in short sentences that summarised what she knew.

Her nephew called and asked if he might drop by, but Aunt Gerda replied that she hadn't the time. The map was approaching its ultimate meaning. It was at a critical stage and would tolerate no interference.

The large planets hold the small ones in place with a firm grip. Satellites follow their predetermined paths. And the strong lines of the dead cross all the others, the double lines, the dotted lines, the coiled lines. Calculation, disappointment, and loss. Aunt Gerda had drawn the beautiful relationships in such light colours that they were hidden by the stronger colours, and perhaps some of them had been erased in the course of her work. Now she drew only words, in short intensive sentences, each of which summarised a truth. Each of them was meant for someone to listen to very carefully.

Did you know it was your fault he died? Do you know that you're not the father of your daughter? That your friend dislikes you?

The map immediately needed alteration and Aunt Gerda drew her first line in gold. It was a terrifying and irresistible mental game that she called 'the fatal words'. It could only be played in the evening by the window. She realised that such words must be uttered only at long intervals, if they were ever really uttered at all. Eight, nine words were sometimes enough for widespread and lasting alterations to the great map on the dining room table. And later, when the time was right, new words for a new listener and once again the picture would change. The effects could be estimated and predicted, like when you play chess with yourself. Aunt Gerda remembered some lines of poetry she'd read as a child.

Frithiof sat with Björn the true
   At the chessboard, fair to view;
Squares of silver decked the frame,
   Interchanged with squares of gold.

She would draw her lines of silver and gold, then wait, perhaps quite a while, then draw another line. She had time, and the material was inexhaustible.

It was early in May. Far into the bright nights she sat by the window and played her great, dangerous game. She didn't light the lamps. The nights were luminous – the transparent, lingering blue that comes with spring. She didn't need to look at the map; she knew it by heart. As she formed and spoke the words, the lines and ovals moved and the colours steadily changed. For the first time in her life, Aunt Gerda had the sweet and bitter experience of power.

When the weather grew warmer, she opened the window, put on her coat, covered her legs with a blanket, and sat in the bay to look out at the city and the strip of open water. Now she could hear footsteps and voices down on the street, every sound clear and distinct. All the passersby seemed to be on their way to the harbour. It seemed to Aunt Gerda that the rooms where she lived no longer enclosed her, they had turned outward and away. The too luminous night was suddenly disquieting and made her sad. She began to think about all the things happening out there right now that she knew nothing about. All the time, every minute, something was happening out there.

Aunt Gerda sat quite still for a long time, then she threw off her blanket and went out into the hall. She called her nephew and asked him if he'd like to come by for a while and talk about his painting, but he was busy and couldn't come. "Painting?" he said. "That was a long time ago, Aunt Gerda. I'm working for Papa now."

She hung up the phone and went into the dining room. Her map was indistinct in the half-light. At the moment, it resembled one of those old representations of the earth seen from the sky, drawn at a time when the known islands were huge but the unknown continents vanishingly small.

Aunt Gerda was a perfectionist. It is possible that she didn't know it or even know that sharp, lovely word. But in her opinion a thing half done was meaningless.

Time had tricked her, dreadful time, which she once again had wasted. Her map was invalid. She rolled it up carefully, fixed it with three rubber bands and wrote, "To be burned unread after my death."

It was a beautiful piece of work, Aunt Gerda thought. It would in fact be a shame if none of them looked at it anyway. She put the map on the highest shelf in the hall closet and closed the window. The footsteps and voices on the street disappeared. Then she lit the lamp above the dining room table and got out her box of shiny pictures and pressed flowers. One by one she laid them on the table and remembered what they looked like. Then, with a single motion of her large, clever hand, Aunt Gerda swept all the pretty pictures back into their box. Several specks of glitter had fallen on the rug and glowed there as blue as the night outside.

Unloading Sand

THE SAND BARGE had anchored beside the granite slope and sacks of cement had been carried ashore. Now they were unloading sand. They'd found a strong young man to handle the wheelbarrow. Again and again he pushed it across the plank, slowly at first but then with long, loping strides that made the plank quake. When he reached the granite he bounced the load up onto the next plank, ran it uphill at a good speed and dumped the sand. As the sand flowed out, he turned away towards the water and scratched his head as if none of this mattered a bit to him and was all just for fun. His back and arms glistened in the sun. His pants were very tight and he wore a greasy little cap, little more than a leaf that had floated down onto his hair. Finally he stretched out one arm, shook the wheelbarrow clean, whipped it around in one easy gesture, clattered back down the rock slope and back over to the barge. As the wheelbarrow rolled across the plank, the only sound was his light steps. Then he spat over the railing as if he owned the whole world and didn't give a damn. He let the others winch up the drum of sand and empty it. He was wonderful.

♦♦♦

She stood beside the cement sacks and watched. Nothing important had happened since she'd learned to do a front flip, and now everything was coming at once, the unloading of the sand and the underwater dynamiting. She couldn't be in two places at once; it wasn't possible. First nothing happens and then nothing happens and then you have to choose. It was hard.

She had got up at four o'clock that morning so she wouldn't lose any of the day and so the whole house would be hers. The early-morning light streamed through the sleeping cottage and across its yellow, varnished summer walls – the walls and floors divided into new spaces by sunshine that would not return all day. It was utterly quiet. She opened the verandah window and the curtain billowed inwards in a great slow surge. The air outside was cold. There were only two meatballs left in the pantry. She tipped them into her mouth from the edge of the plate, licked up the congealed sauce quickly and took bread from the metal breadbox.

The garden smelled of morning, a chilly, expectant smell. The gravel was wet and hurt her feet. With each step she moved further from the cottage, running and chewing, down to the shore and over the stones, jumping and skipping, precise, eating the whole way.

Now he set his feet, grabbed the wheelbarrow and balanced it across the plank again, changing his pace at the fourth step, crossing in a long, swinging gait, then the bounce and the hard clattering sound as the wheelbarrow ran the uphill plank. A new flood of sand spread out and he turned his face towards the water.

She stood behind the cement sacks and envied him with all her might. It was now she had to do it; now or never. She ran onto the boat and hollered down into the hold, "Can I help?" Her voice was too loud, and she was embarrassed.

Two old men stood down in the darkness. They didn't answer. They looked up one time and went on shovelling, the drum was nearly full. She sat down on the deck and waited humbly. He came back with the wheelbarrow and the drum was unloaded into it. He made two more trips and she didn't dare look at him. The third time, they let her go down into the hold.

The daylight vanished as if a door had closed; the vast space lay in deep, cool shadow. The drum came back down. She sank her shovel in the sand and lifted it as quickly as she could. The shovels crossed with a clang, and her hands burned. "You've got to work in rhythm," said one of the old men. "Think about what you're doing." She waited obediently and thought while they filled the drum and winched it up. Shoveling sand is like jumping on rocks, she thought – rhythmic, every movement exact and just enough, never missing, like the guy with the wheelbarrow. The drum came back down. She filled her shovel and raised it, swung it up and over in exactly the second that was hers, lifted and swung and emptied in step with the other two. The three shovels flashed in triple time in the twilight of the hold. It was perfect. Her feet sank deep in the damp red sand. When the drum was full, they stopped shovelling together, leaned on their shovels and rested as they watched the drum swing up on the winch. Up top, he moved to and fro, swaying back and forth across the plank. Again and again the drum came down, first on one side of the keelson and then on the other.

The first charge detonated deeper into the bay. I should have been there to watch. I want to be everywhere. How am I going to live if I always have to choose between two things.

"Second breakfast," the older man said, planting his shovel in the sand.

When she reached the deck, the sunshine was blinding. She walked to the railing and spit in the water, very calmly. Another charge went off, a pillar of water rose above the edge of the woods, unbelievably high, and hung in the air for a long time before it fell. It was completely white. And just at that moment a string of swans flew in over the coast. She had never seen swans flying before, and they called, they sang! A new pillar of water rose towards the sky and the birds crossed it. For one long, lingering moment, there was a great white cross against the blue sky.

She ran across the plank, light and springy, gave a bounce and ran to the side, past the cement sacks and down into the woods. They were quiet and filled with summer warmth, all of June blazed straight down like a fine, glowing rain, but morning mist still drifted across the marsh. She ran into the cool mist and out into the heat again and back into the coolness and through a strong waft of bog myrtle. She threw herself headlong on the moss and the myrtle bent beneath her, right down into the water of the marsh. It would be such an awfully long time until she was fully grown and happy.

The Birthday Party

AT TWENTY PAST THREE, the younger of the Häger sisters lit the candles on the birthday cake. It was already dusk. Her sister took the ice cream out of the refrigerator and began to set it out on a silver platter.

"Couldn't you wait with that?" said Vera Häger. "They'll be here any moment. I think we should greet them together. I'm not used to ..."

Anja went on dishing up the ice cream. "Take them into the sitting room," she said. "Give them some juice. I'll come when I'm done in here."

Vera went out to the front hall. She heard the lift. When it stopped, she opened the door. It was the caretaker. He nodded to her and went up the stairs to the attic. "Excuse me," Miss Häger said. "I thought it was for us. We're expecting visitors, I mean, guests ..." She closed the door and waited behind it. She didn't like the way the caretaker had nodded to her, and there had been no need whatsoever to give him an explanation; she should have kept her mouth shut. Now the lift came up again. She waited for the bell to ring and then threw open the door. There were three children, two boys and a very small girl with her nanny.

"Welcome," said Miss Häger to the nanny. "Our brother's daughter is having a birthday, and her parents are away, and so we thought we – my sister and I – that we ought to throw her a little birthday party ..." The children took off their boots and coats and caps and put them on the floor. The nanny went away.

"And what's your name?" Miss Häger asked. The boys looked away and didn't answer, but the girl whispered, "Pia." The doorbell rang again. It was four children and one mother. More and more children came in and pulled off their winter coats, but their niece didn't come. It was terribly hot in the front hall.

"Come in," said Miss Häger. "Please, go right on into the sitting room, where there's room for everyone. Don't stand in the doorway, go right on in ..." The children went into the sitting room. She clapped her hands and cried, "Now you can start to play! What game would you like to play?" They stared at her without answering. Vera Häger went out into the kitchen and said, "You've got to come, right now, right away. It's not working."

Her sister lifted the platter with the decorated ice cream and said, "What do you mean? What's not working?"

"The party. They're just standing around. I don't think they like me. And Daniela hasn't come."

"Take the ice cream," Anja said. "Go in and give them ice cream. I'll call and find out where she is." She went to the front hall, lifted the receiver and dialled. The line was busy. She tried again. Her sister stood behind her with the platter in her hands and waited.

"Either put the ice cream down or take it in," Anja said.

"Take it yourself," Vera shouted. "Please, take it. Let me call. I'd be so happy to call. I'll keep calling until they answer."

Her sister took the platter and went in. Now it was quite peaceful in the front hall. She dialled the number again and again but it was always busy.

Anja Häger threw streamers over the children as they ate. She was good at throwing streamers. Calmly, carefully, she wove a multicoloured web across the large, dark room. The candles burned quickly in the warmth and made little lakes of wax between the marzipan roses. She blew them out. She passed out balloons and showed them where the lavatory was, and then she went back to the front hall.

"It's still busy," Vera said. "This can't be the wrong day, can it? Do you suppose something's happened?"

"I'll bet they've forgotten to hang up the phone," her sister said.

"Are they playing? Are they having fun?"

"They're eating," Anja said. "You can go in and watch them for a while. I think I'll read for a bit." She went into the bedroom.

Vera Häger stood in the doorway and watched the children. They were no longer stiff. They were all at the table, shoving and pushing. The little girl was building a house out of oranges. A boy was eating ice cream, sitting under his chair. She walked slowly closer. "Are you having fun?" she asked shyly. The children stopped eating and stared at her. For a long moment they stared at each other through the curtain of coloured streamers.

"When I was little," Miss Häger said, "we'd never heard of ice cream. I believe ice cream came along much later. Now don't worry about Daniela, she'll probably be here soon, maybe any minute ..."

Now the children were utterly motionless. The house of oranges fell apart and fruit rolled out across the floor. One of the oranges rolled right up to Vera Häger's feet. She turned and went into the bedroom. Her sister was lying on her bed, reading.

"I don't get it," Vera said. "I just don't get it. Why is there always something wrong with our parties? Not even when it's children ..."

"Read something," Anja said.

The lamp on the night table was green and threw a gentle light across the pillows. They were suddenly conscious of the ticking of the clock.

"We could talk about it," Vera said.

Anja didn't answer. Her glasses reflected the light so her eyes were hidden. She cut several pages of her book, and the book knife made a tinkling sound each time she put it back on the glass top of the night table. The apartment was very quiet.

Vera Häger stood up and opened the door. "They've turned out the light," she whispered.

A lion roared in the sitting room.

"They're playing," Anja Häger said. "They're playing wild animals. Don't look like that. They're having fun."

Suddenly she was infinitely tired of her sister. "Children play," she went on sharply. "They're not like us."

Vera's face collapsed in a grimace and she threw herself onto the bed and wept. Her head was narrow and it was covered with small dry curls at the back that she could probably not see in the mirror. There is no back to her head, Anja thought. Utterly brachycephalic. She put her glasses back on and spoke into her book. "I'm sorry. I just mean that they're having fun. It's a good party. They're eating and roaring at each other. Social life – that's a jungle, smiling and showing your teeth ..."

As she was speaking, she opened the drawer in her night table. Her sister took the tissue automatically, blew her nose, and said, "Thank you. What do you mean, 'showing your teeth'? What are you talking about?"

Anja Häger sat up in her bed, looked at the wall and said, "Social life is dreadful unless you love the people you entertain. People smile with their teeth because they're afraid. Children are honest. They make a dark jungle and roar."

"I don't understand," Vera said.

"Is there anyone," Anja said, "is there one single person we long to spend time with?"

"Are you trying to start an argument?" Vera said.

"It's possible," Anja answered. "But not right now. I'm asking because I'd like to know. We could talk about it."

"We never talk," Vera said. "We just live."

They listened for sounds from the sitting room, and Anja said, "That was a hyena. Wasn't that a hyena?"

Vera nodded. "Does it show I've been crying?"

"It always shows," her sister said. She left the room and walked into the sitting room. The children had taken off their shoes and were crawling under the furniture in the dark. She could hear them snarling at each other. Two of them started fighting and rolled out growling into the weak light from the front hall.

Then the doorbell rang, and Miss Häger turned on the ceiling light and opened the door. The children trooped out and found their coats and boots and caps, the elevator ran up and down, and finally the front hall was empty except for two long black coats. The sitting room floor was covered with trampled streamers and bits of cake. She gathered up the plates and carried them out to the kitchen. Vera sat by the kitchen table, waiting. "You don't need to say it was a great success," she said. "I'm tired of you always saying the same things."

"Oh, so you're tired?" her sister said. "And I always say the same things?" She put the plates carefully in the sink and leaned against the counter, her back to the kitchen. Then she said, "Are you very tired?"

"Very tired," Vera whispered. "What is it you want me to do? What is it that's wrong?"

Anja Häger walked past her sister and touched her lightly on the shoulder. "Nothing," she said. "We'll leave it. It's too late. It's too late to clean up. Let's go to bed and wash up in the morning."

The Sleeping Man

She pulled the telephone into the closet and spoke as quietly as she could. "Are you crazy calling in the middle of the night? There are people here."

"Now listen to what I'm going to say," he said. His voice sounded odd because he was trying to be calm and failing. "I can't give you any names. Don't ask. But someone called to say I have to go and get hold of a key, you know, and check on someone. It's a person they're worried about, but they can't go themselves because they're away."

"What do you mean?" she said. "Whose key?"

"I just said you couldn't ask. I want you to come with me. This is a really important business."

"Now you're making things up again," Leila said.

But the boy shouted, "No! No! It's important! Come with me, please."

"Well, all right, if you really want me," the girl said.

♦♦♦

They walked up an unfamiliar staircase and opened a door with the borrowed key. The hall was full of half-opened boxes; there was a large mirror with a gold frame leaning against the wall. The room beyond was large and unfurnished, with neon lights on the ceiling. He lay on the floor with an embroidered cushion under his head, breathing stertorously. He was a very big man, red in the face, with a lot of brown hair over his eyes. He was old, at least thirty-five.

"Who is he?" she whispered. "Has he been murdered?"

"I told you I don't know," the boy answered. "They called. I told you. I told you on the phone."

"Is he dying?" she said. "You could have woken up other people in the house. And what are we supposed to do now?"

"Call a doctor. Where do you call? Do you know where to call at night?"

"No." She was so cold she was shaking, from the inside.

He went out into the hall, turned around in the doorway and said, "Now, you just stay completely calm. I'll take care of this." A bit later he shouted, "It's 008. I found it in the phone book. They've got it on the cover."

The girl didn't answer; she stared fixedly at the sleeping man. His mouth was open. He looked awful. She moved as far away from him as possible. There weren't any chairs, but of course it would be wrong to sit down.

Ralf was speaking into the phone out in the hall; he was taking care of everything. He'd found a doctor. She let herself sink into resignation, a gentle and pleasant sense of dependence. When he came back she walked over to him and took his hands.

"What's the matter with you?" the boy said, irritated. "It's all fixed. They're coming. I'm to open the street door in ten minutes."

"Then I'm coming with you. I don't want to stay here alone."

"Don't be dumb. Two of us. It would look stupid. Childish."

"You always worry about how it's going to look," she said. "But what about when it's a matter of life and death!?"

He raised his eyebrows and opened his lips, his teeth clenched – a grimace of disgust and contempt. Leila went red in the face. "You said yourself it was important. Why did you drag me along? Why is that fat old man any business of mine?"

He raised his hands and shook them in front of her face. "Don't you understand?" he shouted. "So that, for once, we could do something important together!"

"Don't shout," she said. "You'll wake him."

He started to laugh, leaned against the wall and laughed. The girl watched him coolly and asked, "Did you check the time when you called?" He stopped laughing and left; the front door clicked. Now she was alone with the laboured breathing. It was very near. Sometimes it came closer and sometimes it moved away.

What if he dies when I'm here alone? Why are they always so ugly when they're old? Why can't they deal with their own problems? She kept her eyes on him as she backed out of the room. Softly, she opened the front door and waited. Now they were coming. The lift stopped. The doctor went in without a word to her. He was short and looked annoyed, as if he'd been bothered quite unnecessarily. The front hall smelled of floor wax. She focused her attention on a pattern in the linoleum and stood very still as she waited for the whole thing to be over. If this is the way it's going to be, then I want no part of it. Ugly and hard to understand and sordid. If that's the way the world is, everywhere, all the time, then I don't want any part of it. It's what happens to other people, outsiders, at night ...

Inside, they were talking. And suddenly there was a new voice, indistinct and threatening – the man on the floor. A voice that came from far away, from out of a vast indifference. Then he shouted, with a terrible rage. The girl, Leila, began to tremble. I'll go home, she thought. I'll just open the door and go.

She waited. They came back, and the doctor walked past her again without glancing up, looking just as annoyed.

"Is he getting an ambulance?" she asked.

The boy sat down on the floor and said, "We have to stay here. He's not going to the hospital, but he's going to throw up in the morning."

"What do you mean we're staying here?" the girl shouted. "I won't do it."

He drew up his knees and put his arms around them. "So go, then," he said sullenly. "I'm going to do what they told me to do. You do what you like."

They sat silently and listened to the man breathing in the next room.

"And if he does throw up," the girl said, "we have to find a bowl. Or a bucket."

The boy shrugged his shoulders. He'd put his head down on his knees.

"Will you come in the kitchen and help me look?" she asked, submissively.

"No," Ralf said.

She went into the kitchen and turned on the light. There was a packing case in front of the kitchen counter, and across the address label it said 'Household'. She went back and said, "There's stuff in a packing case, but I can't get it open."

"Really?" said Ralf. "And where the hell do you think I'm going to get my hands on tools in the middle of the night?"

She looked at him, critically and patiently, and said, "If they wrote 'Household' on a box, then they've surely written 'Tools' on another. And they can't have nailed it shut."

They found a hammer and a crowbar. They put a dishpan beside the sleeping man. They found a towel for him, and blankets.

"Do you think we should turn off the light?" Leila wondered. "Is it better if it's light or dark when he wakes up?"

"I don't know. I don't know him. This fluorescent light is horrible; maybe it's better if it's dark."

"I'm not so sure," she said. "If it's dark, then maybe he'll think he's dead, or get scared, and anyway he needs to see where he's supposed to be sick."

"Listen," Ralf said. "It's four o'clock. Why don't we get some sleep?" He spread out a blanket on the hall floor.

"I'll sleep over here in the corner," Leila said.

"And why can't you sleep here next to me?"

"It wouldn't be right."

"And why not? Now, suddenly?"

"Him!" she whispered vehemently. "Him in there. What if he dies?"

The boy rolled himself up in the blanket with his face to the wall. "You're as conventional as your mother," he said. And then, a little later, "Leila, come over here and you'll feel better."

She went to him at once and he spread the blanket over the two of them. It was dark in the hall, but the light from the next room surrounded them, bluish fluorescent light like a hospital ward.

"Ralf?" said Leila.

"Yes."

"What did you mean when you said that we never do anything important together?"

"Nothing much. What I said. We never do anything important, we just get together. Nothing that matters."

"And why does this matter? I think it's nasty."

"I don't know," Ralf said. "I thought it was a good thing, and I wanted you along. Now I'm not so sure. Let's try to sleep."

"I can't sleep." She put her arm around him and whispered, "Maybe you mean that it was a comfort for you to have me along."

"Nonsense," Ralf said. "What do you mean, 'comfort'?"

She pulled her arm back and sat up and said, "Anyway, I was the one who thought of getting him a bowl!"

The man in the next room called out in his sleep, a long cry, as if from a person sinking, lost and distant. They jumped to their feet and grabbed hold of each other.

"Now he's dying!" Leila screamed. "Do something!"

The boy pushed her away and walked stiffly into the room and looked at the man. He had turned and rolled in towards the wall. One hand was pounding the floor, over and over, and now he cried out again, a long, wailing cry. Leila had come into the room and stood by the door listening.

"Go back and lie down," Ralf said. "He's just dreaming."

Her face was worried. She came further into the room and said, "He's scared. He's awfully unhappy." She sat down on her heels beside the sleeping man and tried to look into his face. "It's going to be all right," she said to him. "There's nothing to be afraid of."

The man turned in his sleep and his hand touched hers. Suddenly he took hold of it and held it tight.

"Leila!" the boy burst out.

"Quiet. Be completely quiet," she whispered. "He'll go back to sleep."

The man on the floor held her hand. He stopped moaning and turned his face away.

"See?" she said. "I'm holding his hand."

Gradually his grip relaxed and his hand opened. She stood up and looked at Ralf, made a tiny gesture, a command. He lifted the sleeping man's head and laid it carefully on the cushion, shifted the bowl closer, and spread the blanket to cover him.

"And some water," Leila said.

Ralf went after a glass of water and put it on the floor. It was almost 4.30. They lay down next to each other on the front hall floor and listened to the silence in the unfamiliar building.

"He's scared," Leila explained. "He's terribly scared."

The boy put his arms around her.

"Wake me early," she said. "We've got to find the coffee."

Black-White

Homage to Edward Gorey

His wife's name was Stella, and she was an interior designer – Stella, his beautiful star. Sometimes he tried to sketch her face, which was always at rest, open and accessible, but he never succeeded. Her hands were white and strong and she wore no rings. She worked quickly and without hesitation.

They lived in a house that Stella had designed, an enormous openwork of glass and unpainted wood. The heavy planking had been chosen for its unusually attractive grain and fastened with large brass screws. There were no unnecessary objects to hide the structural materials. When dusk entered their rooms, it was met with low, veiled lighting, while the glass walls reflected the night but held it at a distance. They stepped out onto the terrace, and hidden spotlights came on in the bushes. The darkness crept away, and they stood side by side, throwing no shadows, and he thought, This is perfect. Nothing can change.

She never flirted. She looked straight at the person she was speaking to, and when she undressed at night she did it almost absentmindedly. The house was like her, its eyes were wide open, and sometimes he worried that someone might look in on them from the darkness. But the garden was surrounded by a wall, and the gates were locked.

They often entertained. In the summer, they hung lanterns in the trees and Stella's house resembled an illuminated seashell in the night. Happy people in strong colours moved within this picture in groups or in twos and threes, some of them inside the glass walls and some outside. It was a lovely pageant.

He was an illustrator. He worked mostly for magazines; now and then he did a book jacket.

The only thing that bothered him was a mild but persistent pain in his back, which may have resulted from the excessively low furniture. There was a large black bearskin in front of the fireplace, and sometimes he wanted to lie on it with outstretched arms and legs, bury his face in the fur and roll around like a dog to rest his back. But he never did. The walls were glass, and there were no doors between the rooms.

The large table by the fireplace was also of glass. He was in the habit of laying out his drawings on it in order to show them to Stella before sending them on to the client. These moments meant a great deal to him.

Stella came and looked at his work. "It's good," she said. "Your use of line is perfect. All I'm missing is a dominant element."

"You mean it's too grey?" he said.

"Yes," she said. "It needs more white, more light."

They stood at the low table and he saw his drawings from a distance. They really were very grey.

"I think what it needs is black," he said. "But you need to look at them up close."

Afterwards he thought for a long time about black as a focus. He was uneasy, and his back was worse.

The commission came in November. He went in to his wife and said, "Stella, I've been given a job that really intrigues me." He was happy, almost excited. Stella put down her pen and looked at him. She was always able to interrupt her work without annoyance.

"It's a terror anthology," he said. "Fifteen stories, with black-and-white illustrations and vignettes. I know I can do it. It suits me. It's my kind of thing, don't you think?"

"Absolutely," said his wife. "Are they in a rush?"

"Rush!" he burst out, and laughed. "This isn't some two-bit assignment, this is a serious piece of work. Full pages. They're giving me a couple of months." He rested his hands on her work table and leaned forwards. "Stella," he said gravely, "I'm going to use black as a dominant element. I'm going to do darkness. Grey, well, I'll only use grey when it's like holding your breath, like when you're waiting to be afraid."

She smiled. "It's so nice you've got something you find interesting."

The text arrived, and he lay down on his bed and read the first three stories, no more. He wanted to begin work believing that the best material would come further on and so retain his expectations as long as possible. The third story gave him an idea, and he sat down at the table and cut himself a piece of thick, chalk-white, rag paper with an embossed maker's mark in the corner.

The house was quiet and they weren't expecting guests.

It had been very hard for him to get used to this paper, because he couldn't forget how much it cost. Drawings on less expensive paper tended to be freer and better. But this time it was different. He loved the feel of the pen as it ran across the elegant surface in clean lines and at the same time he relished the barely discernible resistance that brought the lines to life.

It was midday. He closed the curtains, turned on the lamp, and began to work.

◆◆◆

They ate dinner together, and he was very quiet. Stella asked no questions. Finally he said, "It's no good. There's too much light."

"But can't you close the curtains?"

"I did," he said. "But somehow it's still too light. It only gets grey, it doesn't get black!" He waited until the cook had finished serving and gone away. "There aren't any doors in this house," he burst out. "I can't close myself in!"

Stella stopped eating and looked at him. "You mean it's just not working," she said.

"No. All I get is grey."

"Then I think you should find another studio," said his wife. They went on eating, the tension gone. Over coffee she said, "My aunt's old house is standing empty.

But I think there's still furniture in the little attic apartment. You could give it a try."

She called Jansson and asked him to put a heater in the attic room. Mrs Jansson promised to leave food on the steps every day and to make sure the room was clean. Otherwise he'd have to keep house for himself and take a hotplate with him. It took only a few minutes to make all the arrangements.

♦♦♦

When the bus appeared around the bend in the road, he turned earnestly to his wife. "Stella," he said. "It will only be for a couple of weeks, then I can finish up at home. I'm going to concentrate while I'm there. I won't be writing any letters, just working."

"Of course," said his wife. "Now, take care of yourself. And call me from the general store if there's anything you need." They kissed, and he climbed onto the bus. It was afternoon, and sleeting. Stella didn't wave, but she stood and watched until the bus was hidden by the trees. Then she closed the gate and walked back up to her house.

♦♦♦

He recognised the bus stop and the evergreen hedge, but it had grown higher and greyer. He was also surprised that the hill was so steep. The road went straight up, bordered by a confused mass of withered undergrowth and cut by deep furrows where the rain had washed sand and gravel down the slope. The house clung tightly to the hill at an impossible angle just below the crown, and the house, the fence, the outbuildings, the fir trees, all seemed to be holding themselves upright with a terrible effort.

He stopped at the steps and looked up at the façade. The house was very tall and narrow, and the windows looked like arrowslits. The snow was melting, and in the silence he could hear nothing but water dripping in among the firs. He walked around to the back. At the rear of the house was a one-storey kitchen that merged with the hill in a messy, ill-defined rampart of rubbish. Here in the shadow of the firs lay everything the old house had spat out in the course of its life, everything worn out and unnecessary, everything not to be seen. In the darkening winter evening, this landscape was utterly abandoned, a territory that had no meaning for anyone but him. He found it beautiful. Unhurried, he went into the house and up to the attic. He closed the door behind him. Jansson had been there with the heater, a glowing red rectangle over by the bed. He walked to the window and looked down the hill. It seemed to him that the house leaned outwards, tired of clinging to the slope. With great love and admiration, he thought of his wife, who had made it so easy for him to leave. He felt his darkness drawing closer.

♦♦♦

After a long night without dreams, he set to work. He dipped his pen in the India ink and drew calmly – small, tight, skilful lines. But now he knew that grey is only the patient dusk that makes preparation for the night. He could wait. He was no longer working to make a picture but only in order to draw.

In the dusk he walked to the window and saw that the house was leaning outwards. He wrote a letter.

Beloved Stella, the first full page is finished and I think it's good. It's warm here and very quiet. The Janssons had cleaned, and this afternoon they left a canister of food on the steps – lamb wrapped in cabbage, and milk. I make coffee on the hotplate. Don't worry about me, I'm getting along fine. I've been thinking about leaving the margins ragged – maybe I've been too conventional. Anyway, I was right that the dominant needs to be black. Thinking of you, a great deal.

He walked down to the general store and posted the letter after dark. The wind had come up a bit and the fir trees sighed as he walked home. The weather was still warm, snow was melting and running down the hill in furrows of sand and gravel. He had meant to write a longer, different letter.

◆◆◆

The days passed quietly, and he worked steadily. The margins had grown fluid, and his pictures began in a vague and shadowy grey that felt its way inwards, seeking darkness.

He had read the whole anthology and found it banal. There was only one story that was truly frightening. It placed its terror in full daylight in an ordinary room. But all the others gave him the opportunity to draw night or dusk. His vignettes were workmanlike depictions of the people and places the author and the reader would want to see. But they were uninteresting. Again and again he returned to his dark-filled pages. His back no longer ached.

It's the unexpressed that interests me, he thought. I've been drawing too explicitly; it's a mistake to clarify everything. He wrote to Stella.

> You know, I begin to think I've been depicting things for much too long. Now I'm trying to do something new that's all my own. It's much more important to suggest than to portray. I see my work as pieces of reality or unreality carved at random from a long and ineluctable course of events – the darkness I draw continues on endlessly. I cut across it with narrow and dangerous shafts of light ... Stella, I'm not illustrating any longer. I'm making my own pictures, and they follow no text. Some day, someone will explain them. Every time I finish a drawing, I go to the window and think about you.
>
> Your loving husband

He walked down to the general store and posted the letter. On his way home he ran into Jansson, who asked if there was a lot of water in the cellar.

"I haven't been in the cellar," he said.

"Maybe you could have a look," Jansson said. "What with all the rain we've had this year."

He unlocked the cellar and turned on the light. The bulb was mirrored in a motionless expanse of water, as shiny and black as oil. The cellar stairs descended into the water and vanished. He stood still and stared. The walls lay in deep shadow, hollowed out where pieces of the wall had collapsed, and the fallen pieces – lumps of stone and cement – lay half hidden under the water like swimming animals. It seemed to him that they swam backwards, towards the angle where the cellar hallway turned and went further in under the house. I must draw this house, he thought. Quickly. I need to hurry, while it lasts.

He drew the cellar. He drew the back yard, a chaos of carelessly discarded fragments, useless, coal-black, and entirely anonymous in the snow. It was a picture of quiet, gloomy confusion. He drew the sitting room, he drew the verandah. Never before had he been so fully awake. His sleep was deep and easy, the way it had been as a boy. He woke instantaneously, without that half-conscious, uneasy borderland that breaks up sleep and poisons it. Sometimes he slept during the day and worked at night. He lived in a state of furious expectation. He finished one drawing after another. There were more than fifteen, many times more. He no longer bothered with the vignettes.

Stella, I'm drawing the sitting room. It's such a tired old room, completely empty. I draw nothing but the walls and floor, a worn plush carpet, and a wall panel with a repeating pattern. It's a picture of the footsteps that passed through the room, of the shadows that fell on the wall, of the words that still hang in the air – or maybe of the silence. All of that is still here, you see, and that's what I'm drawing. Every time I finish a drawing, I go to the window and think of you.

Stella, have you ever thought about the way wallpaper loosens and opens? It happens according to strict rules. No one can depict desolation who hasn't inhabited desolation and observed it very closely. Things condemned have a terrible beauty.

Stella, do you know what it feels like to see everything grey and cautious all your life and to always try to do your best but all you get is tired? And then suddenly you know, you know with absolute certainty. What are you doing right now? Are you working? Are you happy? Are you tired?

Yes, he thought. She's been working and she's a little tired. She's walking around in her house, getting undressed for the night. She's walking around turning off the lights, one by one, she's as white as blank paper, as white as the innocent challenge of the empty surface, and now she alone gives off light, Stella, my star.

♦♦♦

He was almost certain that the house leaned outwards. Through the window, he could see four steps but not the top one. He put sticks in the snow in order to measure the change in the house's angle of inclination. The water in the cellar did not rise. It didn't matter, anyway. He had drawn both the cellar and the façade. He was now working exclusively on the ragged wallpaper in the sitting room. There was no mail. At times he was not certain which letters he had sent to his wife and which he had only imagined. She was further away now, a picture, a faint pretty picture of a woman. At times, cool and naked, she moved through their large salon of white wood. He found it hard to remember her eyes.

Days and nights and many weeks went by. He worked the whole time. When a drawing was finished, he set it aside and forgot it, continuing at once with a new one, a new white paper, a blank white surface that offered the same challenge, the same limitless possibilities, and an absolute isolation from outside help. Each time he began to draw, he made sure that all the doors in the house were locked. It had begun to rain, but the rain didn't concern him. Nothing concerned him except the tenth story in the anthology. More and more, he thought about this one story, in which the author had subjected daylight to his terror and, against all the rules, enclosed it in an ordinary, pleasant room.

He came closer and closer to the tenth story. It was everywhere, and finally he decided to kill it by drawing. He took a fresh white paper and placed it on the table in front of him. He knew he had to make it visible, the only story in the whole anthology that was genuinely full of horror, and he knew he could illustrate it only one way – it was Stella's living room, her consummate room, where they lived their lives together. He was amazed but utterly certain. He walked around and lit the low lights, all of them, and the windows opened their eyes out towards the illuminated terrace. Beautiful, strange people moved slowly in groups of two or three, and he drew them all, calmly and surely, with small, grey, skilful lines. He drew the room, a terrifying room without doors, bulging with tension, the white walls shadowed with imperceptibly tiny cracks. He let them run on and widen. He drew them all. He saw that the window wall's enormous sheet of glass was on the point of bursting from the pressure from within, and he began drawing it as fast as he could, and at the same time he saw the cleft that opened in the floor and it was black. He worked faster and faster, but before his pen could reach the darkness the room he was drawing turned and crashed outwards to its ruin.

Letters to an Idol

IT WAS EARLY SPRING. Sometimes in the evenings she would stand and gaze at his windows, which had blue curtains. The light behind them was very soft. If the window was dark, she did not leave but stayed where she was and gazed nevertheless. She entertained no hopes; she was simply paying respect. The street's impersonal loneliness, the cold, and the long walk home were also tributes. She had never seen him. She had a blue scrapbook into which she pasted every article about him from the newspapers, weeping with anger when what they said wasn't kind. The pictures were often blurry and did not do him justice. His books were always about love. She was proud of the fact that he dared to write as he did, without the least concession to the changing times. He knew that longing and shyness and dreams are the essential nature and privilege of love, together with its patient capacity to wait and to forgive. He wrote a new book almost every year. She owned all of them, including the earliest works of his youth.

She never wrote to him. It gave her a secret advantage and the chance to continue loving – dreamily, stubbornly, and with greater and greater experience. Her rituals were free of the pathetic hope of being noticed. She could open the telephone catalogue and just stare at his name until her eyes filled with tears. She drew strength from the quiet perseverance that is a mature woman's dignity and pride. She had not been a mature woman for very long.

The snow began to melt, and he published his most beautiful book. The critics were cruel. The reviews were so terrible that she couldn't paste them into her scrapbook. She burned them and wept. This happened at the beginning of April, and something in the relationship between them changed in the weeks that followed. Hesitantly, then with earnest conviction, she dared to believe that he needed her. She understood him. She lived her life in accordance with his books, and everything he said was an echo of what she herself had felt, as completely as if they had called to one another.

She wrote to him. The letter was stiff and almost without adjectives. She told him that she considered the recent criticism unjustified. Awkwardly and with restraint, she tried to express what his books had meant to her and, finally, with a womanly wisdom that was surprising for her age, she did not provide her own address. He gets thousands of letters, she thought, and her pride touched both of them. I don't want to be a letter that has to be answered. I want to be the anonymous correspondent that he can't stop wondering about.

When she had mailed the letter, her sense of liberation was so great that she wanted to run and jump, so she ran into the park and rushed back and forth between the trees where no one could see her. She kicked open a channel for meltwater in the wet snow and dug in the sand with her hands.

For several days she hardly thought about him, and not once did it cross her mind to go and stare at his window. It was almost like deserting him, not really but almost, and in the end she started reading his books all over again in chronological order as a declaration of fidelity. Through all of them, men and women circled one another in worshipful reticence. Through hundreds of pages they approached their ultimate but always undescribed union.

One night she woke breathless with fear and knew that she had waited too long. He had forgotten her. She got up to write a new letter, in which she pleaded with him to pursue his muse in spite of everything. Reviews mean nothing, she wrote. What they think is utterly meaningless, they don't understand. They don't understand how courageous it is – at this moment, when love is cheap and vulgar and lacking in mystery – for someone to dare to defend purity. She tried to explain that he had taken what had become mere anatomy and built it into a temple, but the sentence became so odd that she scratched it out and started a new letter. And in the end she gave him her address, which she wrote in tiny letters at the very bottom of the page. She ran to the letter box on the corner and stood and gazed at it. The slot was half open. It was like a mouth that was ready to bite her. She hesitated, then quickly tossed in the letter and the cover fell shut with a bang. And in that second she knew with sober certainty that she had now abandoned herself to disappointment.

♦♦♦

He answered at once. He did in fact answer so quickly that she never had time to prepare herself to wait. There was the letter lying on the front hall rug, and it was from him. She had imagined that if he wrote – supposing he actually did write some day when he had the time or was in the right mood or had decided to get some chores out of the way – then she would take the letter to some pretty place, perhaps by the sea, and open it there. But she ripped it open right there in the hall without a thought to saving the envelope and read it quickly, breathlessly, skimmingly – a whole page, handwritten. He was chivalrous. His letter was like his books. He had taken time with it, and it was for her alone. He thanked her and assured her that his view of women would never change, that he would always see them as beautiful and pure.

The world changed, imperceptibly but utterly. She moved differently, lingeringly. Absentmindedly, without plan or calculation, she would look at her image in mirrors or shop windows, absorbing herself in her own femininity. What a lot happens, she thought, gratefully. So many changes. I haven't had the time to be unhappy for weeks. Her job grew unimportant – for what significance can a job have in these circumstances? She did it automatically, dreamily. Elegant, old-fashioned words wafted through her mind, and she amused herself with beautiful gestures or simply by sitting still with her hands in her lap. It was a happy, slow time. Once again she was using him to live a more concentrated life. She did not write to him. She partook of the uncommon happiness of delaying what she longed for. She knew that a rose lay at her feet, but she did not pick it up.

There came a period of rain, a long spring rain that took the snow with it. The ice broke up. And finally she wrote again, at night, very quickly and better than she'd ever written before.

He didn't answer. Time passed and he didn't answer. There is a difference between silence that anticipates and silence that is final.

Only now – in a state of disappointment so great that it denied her even the comfort of grieving – only now did she feel she understood what it was she hoped for. It was nothing less than to become the person he wrote to when he was feeling low, when he couldn't work, when he doubted himself and felt alone. It could have been a long, beautiful correspondence, whose meaning and beauty lay in the fact that they never met, not a single time until one of them died. All through history, the artist and a woman have exchanged such letters, precious, inspirational letters that have given posterity a completely new view of the artist and his work. And possibly of the woman. She had spoiled everything, and it was a realization she couldn't bear.

She took a taxi and ran up the stairs and rang his bell. It was eight o'clock in the evening. She had forgotten to make herself pretty, but for the moment she thought of nothing at all, just went straight in and said earnestly, "I'm the one who wrote to you." Her gravity was almost stern and gave her a new dignity that was all her own. As she gazed at him, all the blurred newspaper portraits slid together, quick as a deck of cards, and he no longer looked like an author. He said, "It was nice of you to come and visit," and he took her coat.

The room was large. The blue curtains went from wall to wall and all the way down to the soft, purple floor. All the colours were deep and restrained and the lamplight was soft and flattering. It was an impersonal room, with a sense of lofty seclusion and luxury. The only thing that didn't belong was a large, soiled tiger skin. Its mouth agape as if it were gasping for air. She walked around it to the sofa.

"Would you like a drink?" he said.

She sat down. "Yes, thank you," she said. The sofa was much lower than she had estimated, and she nearly lost her balance and felt ridiculous. In the blink of an eye, she lost her dignity, the tiny but passionate dignity that had graced her for a few moments. She giggled and started digging in her purse. He mixed sweet vermouth and ice water without asking what she wanted. For himself, he poured some lemon juice.

Everything was ebbing away. The ice cubes tinkled in her glass as she shook it slowly and searched for words. She said what she had already written – that his last book was the finest thing he'd ever done, and he replied that he was pleased to hear her say so, that he was very glad she liked it. Now the ball was in her court again. She clinked her ice cubes and said with enormous effort, "There are things that can be treated so many different ways, like this question of purity, which is so essential. I mean, whatever happens and however things evolve, you know, towards absolute freedom – people getting freer and freer, doing whatever they want and saying and showing whatever they want – but I don't think it's right. It's not pretty. And words are important."

"You're right," he said. "Words are important." He was very attentive. Actually he had terribly small eyes and his lashes were perfectly black. She went on hurriedly. "What you describe in your books is a thing that has almost been lost. It belongs in another century! I mean, isn't it true that people talk to death things that are so fragile and fine that they shouldn't be talked about at all?"

He looked thoughtful and she added vehemently, "I mean, it gets all turned around. It turns people off, and isn't that a shame?"

"That's an interesting thought," he said slowly and as if from a great distance. He had stood up and now he asked if she'd like to have some music. She said bluntly, "Yes." He asked what kind of music and she said it didn't matter. "But I have everything," he said. "Whatever in the world you'd like. You have only to say."

At that moment, all she could remember was Beethoven and the Beatles, so she said curtly, "You decide. The way you decided my drink."

A clear, chilly, gentle music streamed forth and filled the room, thoughtful and impassive. The decision not to speak altered her face, which shrivelled and grew childish. She was no longer trying to please.

"Now you're tired of me," he said. "It was wrong of me, pouring you vermouth. May I offer you a whisky or Cognac instead, or is there something else you'd like?"

"No, no, not at all," she answered quickly, half suffocated by remorse and confusion. Why doesn't he talk the way he writes? He's friendly, but it's the wrong kind of friendliness. It doesn't mean anything. That's the way you comfort someone who doesn't count, someone who's behaved badly and isn't even really grown up.

"Is that skin from Africa?" she said.

"India, maybe," he said. Now he's withdrawing again, that was wrong. You don't make small talk with a writer, you talk about essentials. I've only been thinking of myself, not about him at all. They both began speaking at once, at exactly the same instant. They stopped and looked at each other.

"I beg your pardon," he said. "You were saying ...?"

"No, it was nothing."

"No, please go on ..."

"I was just thinking," she said. "What does a person do, what does an author do if he's misunderstood and gets depressed and can no longer write? It must be dreadful to get bad reviews, and how many people are there who understood what it's like, and how important it is not to ..." His face closed and she went silent with shame, a shame she could not understand or control, and the music had reached its finale and so it stopped as well.

It could all have been indescribably awful, but now the author extended his hand and touched hers, one short second, and asked respectfully which of his books she had read. She drew a deep breath and looked straight at him with that special sadness that only adoration can produce. "All of them," she said. "Every book you've written. They have their own shelf and I never mix them with ordinary books. I live by them, though it's not easy. I believe in them. I'm your disciple."

The astonishing, archaic word "disciple" hung there between them, as palpable and exacting as the silence that followed his strange and chilly music. Now I need not say anything more, she thought. This was right, he liked it.

Finally he spoke the way he wrote, and only to her. With precision and respect he said, "My dear friend." And these unusual words hovered in the air, filled the room, and were impossible to follow. It was too much, it was overwhelming. In blind ecstasy and terror she grasped his hand, quite hard, and pressed it to her mouth. A terrible embarrassment overcame them. They stood up simultaneously and heard someone open the hall door and come into the room. He spoke quickly and very softly. "You are my protectress. I shall not forget you." With a cautious grip on her elbow, he escorted her out into the front hall and helped her on with her coat. He opened the door. The person who had come in was large and tall, but she never saw him, only his boots, and now she was out on the stairs and then on the street, and the night was bright and quite warm. She walked up one street and down another and thought, My dear friend, My protectress, I shall not forget you. After such words, there was no longer any need to speak to each other ever again, and with great sincerity she decided that this was in fact a beautiful thing. She went home and went to bed and slept the whole night as peacefully as people do when a difficult work is completed – and completed with honour.

The next morning was a Sunday. She lay in bed for a long time and tried to recall every remark, every silence, every gesture, all the colours and the lighting and the chilly music, but it all flowed together, further and further away, as unreal as in his books. She rolled over in bed and fell back asleep with her arms wound tightly around her body in a caress of quiet respect and expectation.

A Love Story

HE WAS A PAINTER. For years, art exhibitions of all kinds had bored or depressed him. But when he walked into a tiny connecting room at the Biennale in Venice, he stopped abruptly and was suddenly wide awake. He stood in sincere and undivided admiration of a representational, almost naturalistic sculpture of a woman's buttocks – in pink marble, cut off a bit above the knee as in classical representations of the torso, but also just above the navel. The sculptor had not cared about anything other than this free-standing, consummate posterior. Certainly he knew the Callipygian Venus, Venus with the beautiful buttocks who lifts her garment to assure herself with a glance over her shoulder that her derrière is her loveliest feature. But here the buttocks were wholly without props. They stood alone in pink marble, the rounded fruits of the artist's love and insight.

The sculpture stood on a black pedestal maybe one metre high, in a room with grey walls and northern light, a tiny room between two doors. The wall opposite the window, the only one that offered enough space for a painting, was occupied by a work in scorched brown plastic. The sculpture was, in other words, completely undisturbed. Surrounded by dark colours, lit by cool daylight, it was like a lustrous pink pearl. The light embraced the marble and filled it with translucence. The painter thought this beautiful backside was the most sensual and respectful symbol of woman he had ever seen. People walked through the room from time to time but hardly paused. They walked on, while the painter lingered deep in thought, lost at last in the adoration of a work of art. He had always wondered what it would feel like.

These buttocks had almost sumptuous contours, which were at once restrained and austere. The two halves rested together like a peach around its groove, the one slightly raised towards the curve of the hips. The shadows were soft, like those on a youthful cheek, and despite the sculptor's clearly sensual delight his work was oddly out of reach. This backside could have been a symbol of eternity.

The painter didn't touch the marble. He stood there for so long that the shadows altered on the sculpture as if the woman had imperceptibly moved and turned towards him.

Suddenly the painter left the room and went to ask the price.

He learned that the sculptor was Hungarian, and that the sculpture was very dear.

It is unusual to feel an irreducible and absolute desire, a desire so strong that it sweeps all else aside, for once in your life to be filled with an overwhelming craving. The painter wanted to own these marble buttocks and take them home with him to Finland.

He walked back to the hotel, a very small hotel in one of the narrow streets behind the San Marco palace. The stairs were dark after the blinding sunlight, and he walked upwards slowly, step by step, trying to formulate what he would say. Aina was lying on the bed. It was very hot, and she had nothing on.

"How was it?" she said.

He said, "The same old stuff. Have you been out?"

She reached across the table and showed him a handful of trinkets, seashells and glittering glass, and told him it had cost her almost nothing. "Almost nothing at all!" she repeated. She put the necklaces on her stomach and laughed playfully.

He looked at her, concerned.

"But they weren't expensive," she assured him. "You know I don't throw money away." She came to him and he put his arms around her the usual way. His hands rested on her warm buttocks, and he couldn't say a word about the sculpture in pink marble.

When the evening cooled, they went out into the city. They always walked the same way, across the Piazza San Marco, and Aina repeated what she'd heard him say those first few days. She talked about old gold and marble's patina and their daring in having built the way they had. And then she turned to him and said, in her own way, "How they must have loved what they were doing, and loved each other! Otherwise, how could they have produced all this?"

He kissed her, and they walked on. They went to the restaurant they liked, which was cheap. They ate spaghetti and drank red wine. There were tourists, but it was genuine all the same. Outside, the evening quickly turned dark blue.

"Are you happy?" Aina said, and he answered honestly that he was. He did not confuse what he longed for with his gratitude for what he had. Extreme desires have their own sanctuary. But while they walked the narrow streets and crossed the bridges, while they ate and talked and gazed at one another, the whole time, the whole evening, he calculated and tried to get the numbers to add up, counted all the cities they hadn't yet seen and realised that if he bought the beautiful statue they would have to go back home at once.

"What are thinking about?" Aina wanted to know, and he replied, "Nothing in particular."

They left the restaurant and wandered through Venice along the same lanes and across the same bridges. The city was all curves and labyrinths, they always came back to the same places, and they never knew where they were.

"The palaces are mirrored in the canals!" Aina exclaimed. She was a little drunk. "Look at the green seaweed creeping up the walls. It's all decaying. That palace is slowly sinking, one row of windows after another ... Do you love me?"

"I do," he said.

"But you're thinking about something else the whole time."

"I am," he said.

She stopped on the bridge to look at him. She was having a little trouble focusing. "Tell me what you're sad about," she said slowly and with exaggerated solemnity. She looked comical and earnest, standing there on too-high heels that altered the natural angle of her legs and forced her knees forwards, with her tourist jewellery and the locks of hair on her forehead rolled up individually on pins and her ridiculous little purse. Her overwhelming femininity struck him dumb. People walked over the bridge and past them, slowly in the warm darkness. That's what's so remarkable, he thought absentmindedly. There's no traffic. They just walk, nothing but the sound of footsteps. "Aina," he said, "I'm thinking about a sculpture I saw at the Biennale. It's a thing in marble, and I'd like to have it. Own it. Take it home with us. But it's expensive."

"You mean you want to buy a piece of art?" said Aina, flabbergasted. "But you can't be serious!"

"It's beautiful," he said angrily. "A fine piece of work."

"My God," Aina said. She started walking again, and they continued down the bridge steps.

"It's expensive," he repeated vehemently. "The whole grant, all of it. If I buy it, we'll have to go home."

They walked past several closed palaces that had their feet in the canal. Gondolas glided by with lanterns and tourists and singing gondoliers, and the moon had risen. She let all this melancholy, heart-rending beauty flow into her and mix with her familiar love for the painter, and suddenly it felt completely natural to say, "But if you want that sculpture so terribly badly, then it's probably best to buy it, don't you think? Because otherwise you'll just go around thinking about it?" She stopped and waited for his gratitude, and when he embraced her she closed her eyes and thought, How easy it is to love.

"And what's it a sculpture of?" she whispered.

"A torso," he said.

"A torso?"

"Yes. Well, actually it's buttocks. In pink marble."

She pulled back and repeated, "Buttocks? Just buttocks?"

"You need to see it," he said. "You can't understand unless you see it." He pulled her to him and tried to hold her while he described it, searching for words, but she didn't want to listen. They walked home in silence. They reached the Piazza and their own street, and the moon shone but didn't help at all. What a banal story, he thought. I know what she's going to do. She'll get undressed behind the screen and get into her bed backwards so I won't be able to see her behind. It's all so stupid.

They entered their hotel room. They didn't usually turn on the light in the evening, because the glow from the Piazza spread into their street and gave the room a lovely reddish half-light. Down on the street, people walked by singing, *bellissima, bellissima* ...

"Listen," he said. "They're not tourists. They live here. And they're not coming home from a party. They just feel like singing ..." It was a remark he made just for her, because she would like it, but all she said was, "Yes, I know."

Now it's bad, he thought. If I go to her bed, that's bad, and if I don't that's even worse. I can't tell her I don't want the sculpture. I can't do anything at all. The painter was so tired he just sat on the edge of his bed, exhausted. Aina undressed behind the screen, quickly and quietly. And then she moved about the room for a long time, fussing and arranging, and finally she came to him with two glasses of wine. She was wearing her robe. She gave him one of the glasses and sat down on the floor in front of him. "I've been thinking," she said earnestly, almost sternly.

"Have you?" he said submissively, already trembling with relief.

She leaned forward and studied his face with wrinkled eyebrows. "We'll steal it," she said. "We'll just go in and simply steal it. I'm not afraid."

He saw her face in the drifting light from the Piazza and saw that she was serious. He thought quickly and said, "Do you think we can get away with it?"

"Of course," she cried. "We can get away with anything. It's the ground floor, I know that, and there's a park outside. We'll cut open a pane of glass with a diamond. We'll have to buy a diamond, just a little one. Can you carry it, or do we have to get a wheelbarrow?"

"Fantastic," the painter said. He stood and went to the window and listened to the footsteps on the street. He felt like laughing. Suddenly he felt like decamping right then, at night, taking his woman and travelling on to anywhere. He turned to her and said, gravely, "I don't think we should. We'll have to live without the sculpture. Think of the sculptor. He's Hungarian. How will he know that it's us who's got his sculpture in our studio in Finland? And he probably needs the money."

"That's true," Aina said. "Such a shame." She put her robe on a chair and got into bed.

They lay side by side, and she said, "What are you thinking?"

"About the sculpture," he said.

"Me too," she said. "Tomorrow we'll go and look at it together."

The Other

THE FIRST TIME was in the milk shop as he stood looking at the display of cakes under the glass counter, completely indifferent to the ingratiating pastries but eager to avoid looking at the clerk. Suddenly, and with dreadful clarity, he saw himself. Not in a mirror. He actually stood beside himself for an instant and thought quietly, There stands a skinny, timid, stoop-shouldered fellow buying cheese and milk and a piece of ham. The apparition lasted only for a second.

Afterwards he was upset, and on the way home he wondered if he had strained his eyes with the latest lettering – the text was extremely small. He put his food between the windows where it was cold and sat down at his drawing table to finish the commission. He opened his drawing instruments and filled his finest pen with ink. And there it was again, powerfully. With a sharpening of all his senses, he stood beside himself and observed a man drawing tiny, fine, parallel lines, a man he did not like but who aroused his interest. This time, it lasted a little longer, perhaps five seconds.

He felt a slight chill, but his hands weren't shaking, so he finished the job, cleaned it up and put the sheet in an envelope. The whole time he was writing the address, licking the stamps, closing the metal clasps, he was on the verge of gliding away to stand alongside himself, watching a man prepare a parcel. It was a very close thing. He put on his hat and coat to go to the post office. Down on the street, he started to tremble and clenched his jaws so tightly that they hurt. Nothing happened at the post office. He cashed a money order and bought some stamps. He decided to take a walk along the harbour, although it was raining and quite cold – a calm, purposeful man taking a quick walk to relax and dispel his thoughts. Exhaustion sometimes produces phenomena that can be easily explained. They vanish if you leave them alone and refuse to let yourself be frightened.

He avoided looking at the people he passed. The wind was blowing from the water, and the warehouses along the waterfront were closed. He walked and walked, trying to occupy his thoughts with something of interest. He could think of nothing but lettering. He tried to capture and hold onto the tiniest scrap of usable thought, but the only thing he really cared about was lettering. In the end, he let his troubled mind rest in a large, quiet surface of letters, a text arrangement of perfect beauty to which the key was distance and balance. That's the way it is with letters – distance and space are what matters. He usually started inking from the bottom up so that he wouldn't be distracted by the meaning of the words.

By the time he reached the promontory, he felt calmer. A very long time ago, when he still suffered from ambition and disappointment, someone had said that he didn't love his letters and that it showed. The remark had hurt and troubled him. He had seen text arrangements that were considered vivid and expressive. They struck him as clumsily done – not even retouched. For him, the stamp of quality was objectivity and purity. Lettering and mathematics have exactly the same potential for perfection. There can be only one right answer.

Now he had the wind at his back. He passed a sign at the ferry and noticed in passing that the letters were awkward and ugly. His attention slid away and a quick stab of anxiety swept over him. He tried to look at boats, joints in the stone pier, iron rings, moorings, anything at all, the way a person entering a strange room searches for conversation pieces among the room's indifferent objects. Finally he tried to think about the daily newspaper, about reports of great and frightening significance, but all he saw was a great blurry text of stocky typefaces, black in the headlines and otherwise completely unreadable. He started to run. It came closer. It came back.

He stopped and took a big step to one side and they walked on together. This time it was very distinct and lasted for maybe a minute. A minute is a long time. He saw his own overcoat flapping about his legs in the wind and caught a glimpse of a pinched profile under his hat, the profile of a gentleman who cared about nothing, a gentleman who was out walking because he didn't want to go home. His interest was mixed with contempt, and he wondered if the man who walked beside him was afraid and if he too felt contempt. He felt warm and vaguely impatient.

The phenomenon ended and all he saw was the wet asphalt. Mechanically, he went on walking. His heart pounded rapidly and hard. No one had ever looked at him that way before, with such interest and intensity. He walked into the park and sat down on a bench as if he were waiting for someone. His heart was still pounding and he didn't dare raise his eyes from the ground. Nothing happened. He waited for a long time and nothing happened. He did not try to understand, he only waited. When it began to rain, he rose in disappointment and went home. It was not yet evening, but he fell asleep at once, hugely tired, and slept straight through to morning.

♦♦♦

He woke in an odd mood that he didn't recognise as expectant. He dressed himself with great care, shaved, tidied his room – listening the entire time. It occurred to him that he might be listening for the doorbell or the telephone, so he turned off both. He did not work today. He moved as quietly and slowly as possible, back and forth across the room, and as he moved, he fussed with the small objects set out for use or decoration, moving them about and putting them back, listening uninterruptedly. He took two pretty glasses out of the cupboard and put them back again. The day passed.

It came at dusk, as he looked out the window. Again they stood side by side, utterly still so as not to upset the balance in this remarkable displacement, confusion, or whatever other name might be given to what they were experiencing. He felt the same sympathetic contempt, but a new warmth and quickness pulsed through the sympathy he felt for the person he was visiting. He was strong. A few minutes later, he was alone again, but for those few minutes he had been very happy.

He was alone all that day and all that week. He prepared himself, but nothing happened. Disappointment and anticipation became almost an obsession. He thought about nothing but the opportunity to stand to the side. That's what he called it in his head, standing to the side. He returned to the places where they had been together and waited for a long time. He tried to remember books about doppelgängers and dual personalities but could no longer recall their names, and he didn't want to consult bookshop assistants and librarians. The meeting he was preparing for was extremely personal and secret. It could not be hastened or explained. All he could do was render himself utterly, impersonally receptive. He knew for certain that he was a receiver – he radiated nothing but expectation. So he waited.

Finally he succeeded. He stepped out of himself without even feeling contempt for the person he'd left. They stood there side by side as they'd done before and gazed out the window. He allowed delight and alertness to wash through him like a warm wave. His hands burned, his totally new hands. The whole time he stared out the window. Then the two of them glided back into one another. This happened with a sense of weary reluctance and left behind it a feeling of disappointment, flaccid and ghastly. He was alone in the room. He ran to the door and back to the window, at his wit's end from abandonment. Again and again he thought, bitterly, He doesn't look at me any more, why doesn't he look at me? He remembered the story about the doppelgänger who killed himself. He couldn't work.

The rain had stopped, and the weather was chilly and clear. He put on his boots and a warm coat, left the house and took a bus out to where the city came to an end. Day after day, he wandered around in the borderland where the buildings thin out and lose themselves in arbitrary ugliness. He returned to the area every morning and walked incessantly, occasionally resting on a bench or in some café by a railway crossing or a factory. The impersonal, undefined environment was perhaps a preparation for his meeting the other, perhaps a challenge. Spring came closer, a work in progress, much like the area he wandered through, as muddy and melancholy in every way. He didn't know what he felt for the one he expected, for the one he made a place for and opened himself up to – at times he was an enemy, at times a friend. In the cafés, he sometimes ordered two cups of coffee, which was also a challenge. Sometimes someone tried to speak to him, more often here than in the city. When that happened, he would immediately stand up and leave.

In these unpopulated, half-built, discarded outlands, he felt he could see the city's discharge, the wave of dirty foam that flows over the rim and settles. Letters and words had also been flushed out; he could see them everywhere in signs, posters, placards. Every fence and wall, even the trees, carried black words that pursued him. But he didn't read them. Chalk and knives and tar had written words that screamed at him and drove him on down a gauntlet between fences and walls and trees, all bearing the impress of the written word. He walked in circles and found distance and space nowhere, balance nowhere. He had begun to think of himself in the third person, "he". He wanders here, waiting, he is waiting for me, walking among these horrible words and these great fields lined with wooden houses and rubbish tips. He walks quickly past the people he encounters and waits only for me to see him and take him under my wing. He passes long murals of barracks and streets and crossroads, again and again, and they are all alike, ceaselessly and sadly repeating, like lost time.

The last snow melted. One day he walked through a thin grove of birches somewhere between two highways, and there, finally, he stood to the side. In a state of great joy, he stood ready to walk on, but now it was not only his hands that felt alive but also his head, his stomach, all of him. His whole body burned with an enormous unused power. Behind the copse of trees by the main road, he could see large black letters. He wanted to read them and understand them, and he started walking, just then I started walking. I wanted to move on, and I started to walk, faster and faster, I hadn't known I could feel like this. I was mad with joy and impatience and I knew there wasn't much time and there was too much to do. I looked back one single time, and there he came, running, stumbling across the marshy ground, stoop-shouldered, his mouth agape as if he were calling to me to wait. I had no time for him, because he was only one person but I was seeing him. I did not reach out to him, I'm sure I didn't, but he threw himself forwards, towards my hand and grabbed it, and before I had time to despise him it was too late – we were just one person, a single figure standing stock-still beneath the birches, waiting.

In Spring

EARLY IN THE MORNING, before it gets light, the snow ploughs circle the block. With a dull scraping noise they dig out broad paths along the pavements, and nothing gives a deeper sense of restfulness and warmth than listening to snow being cleared as, half awake, I turn over and go back to sleep. Sometimes I lie crossways in my big bed and sometimes diagonally. I like having plenty of space.

More and more snow cascades down in the darkness and is just as steadily scraped away. During the day, fog rolls in from the sea. We've had snow-fog for a very long time now and have walked around in twilight.

Last night there was thunder, probably thunder, a couple of powerful crashes, not a rumble, but more like tremors that went right down through the building. In the morning, the sky was completely clear, filled with a hard, exuberant light, and later that day the snow began to melt. There was a continuous shifting and changing outdoors, snow tumbling from the buildings in great white clutches, water clattering on metal roofs, meltwater streaming, and the whole time that powerful, challenging light. I went out on the street. The sound of rushing water was almost violent, babbling and flooding across the pavement and the street amid the thudding of the falling snow.

In this naked light, all of winter's traces are visible not least in a face. Everything becomes distinct and turns outwards, exposed, penetrated by the light. People come out of their holes. Perhaps they've survived the winter in flocks or maybe alone, willy-nilly, but now they appear and make their way to the harbour, the way they always do.

It was easier to walk past each other protected by cold and darkness. Now we stop and tell each other spring has come. I say, "Drop in sometime," but I don't mean it. And he says, "How are you doing?" without meaning anything special – I think. We are stuck with each other because we're both on our way to the corner and there are no side streets.

So much water dripping and running, and how everything sparkles and dazzles! Now everything will start to grow again, all of it, all over again. Where does it get the energy? It's just fantastic this business about always getting another chance, and I ask, "Are you with someone these days, or are you living alone?" "No," he says matter-of-factly, "I'm not seeing anyone." And I say that's too bad, now it's spring. So we exchange information that has a certain significance, if very little, and we part with our dignity intact. I walk on across the square, taking note of all the rushing and gushing. The water in the gutters is almost clean, and beyond the quay the sun is boring into the ice, which burns away in fine, needle-like formations.

I've heard that it's thunderstorms that break up the ice, but I don't know why. I could call him. He could have kept me company down to the harbour. Or maybe not. There are big pools of meltwater where the storm sewers empty into the harbour, full of trash and plastic and all the filth and refuse of the city, bubbling and glittering in the sunshine, bobbing cheerfully against the harbour wall, though maybe some of it will drift out by and by and float away and big waves will take it in hand, maybe.

I drift along the shore that encloses the city where I live until I come to the last point of land, and there they are, all of them, the black winter people on this blindingly bright spring day. One by one, each of them separately, they sit on the steps on the hillside and turn their faces upwards, as stiff and solemn as birds. Maybe he should have come with me after all. They stand out on the docks, just stand there quite still, each one alone. The ice is quite dark. It looks soft and yielding. The entire landscape rests on a threshold or perhaps a wave, ready to glide over the top and make a decision. This is roughly my train of thought, hasty and confused. Then I decide to call tomorrow, not today.

That night I hear the snowploughs. The morning is overcast and very cold. I don't call. After all, what would I say? It starts snowing again, the room is filled with a pleasant twilight, the snowdrifts grow all around and smother all sounds except the scraping of the ploughs down on the street. I fall back to sleep. So goes the long spring, here, in our country.

The Silent Room

AFTERWARDS, THEY WENT UP TO THE FLAT. The police had been there, but he himself was still in the hospital. He lived on the third floor, and his name plate was like his neighbours', perfectly ordinary. He had a Christmas wreath on the door – green lingonberry sprigs in plastic. There was no post on the hall rug. They came into a large living room with southern sun and wall-to-wall carpet, modern wallpaper, but inherited furniture. It was all very tidy, the bathroom as well. He had a refrigerator and a washing machine in the kitchen, and the cupboards smelled clean.

"Can you figure it out?" she said. "I just can't understand why he did it. And as old as he is! They almost never do it at that age." She was large and level-headed and was wearing an attractive suit she had made herself. Her brother shrugged his shoulders and walked over to the window. The view was pleasant, a corner of the park and, further off, an open school playground. The room was very quiet. It has the same silence I have at home, he thought. Untouched, somehow. He went to the cupboard and took out the dressing gown and put it into the valise they'd brought with them.

"Slippers," his sister read from the list. "Toiletries and pyjamas. Oh yes, they've put him in a private room and they said he wanted his glasses ..."

At the back of the cupboard was a large box. It was full of unopened cartons and rolls of leather and strange tools.

"What are you doing?" she said. "What's all that?"

"I think it's bookbinding tools," he said. Everything was new, the price tags were still on. He looked for the slippers under the sofa, but the only thing there were some flat boxes and a yellow wooden chest. Parts for model ships – a caravel, the *Cutty Sark*. He pulled out the chest.

"What are you doing?" she asked again. "Can't you find the slippers?"

He undid the hasp. It was a complete set of carpenter's tools. "They're brand new," he said. "He's never used them."

"So it seems," she said. "But I ought to get some groceries before they close. And I don't think we ought to search through his things any more than we have to." She went to get the toiletries and found his glasses in the drawer of his night table. Everything was neat and orderly, linens and underwear in even, carefully folded piles. She went back to the living room. Her brother had opened the desk drawer. "And what are you searching for now?" she said.

"I'm not searching," he said. "I'm just looking." He wanted to say, I'm looking for him, I'm trying to understand. But they had never talked to each other that way.

Some envelopes. One of them said "Receipts", another "Fire Insurance". Forms. Directions for use.

"There's not much to see in here," she said quietly. She put the last items into the valise and closed it. "I think that's everything. Now I need to get going and take care of dinner."

"Off you go," he said. "I can take the bag to the hospital. We're not headed the same way, anyhow."

She looked at him and he explained. "I'm a little tired. I think I'll sit here for a while and look at a book."

"You're always tired," his sister said. "You should see a doctor. You're not exactly getting any younger. Goodbye then, and don't forget to leave the keys with the caretaker."

Now the room grew as quiet as before, a soft, quilted, absolute silence. Maybe it was due to all the rugs and draperies and overstuffed furniture, and of course the books. Why does someone ask for his glasses when he doesn't ask for any books? But maybe it was his distance glasses. He read the spines. Book Circle books and gift books. Inherited books. Famous books. He took out one of them and saw that the pages hadn't been cut. He took out several more; almost none had been cut. Behind them, against the wall, was another layer of books – of an entirely different sort. Orchid cultivation, how to lay a patio, how to build a ship in a bottle. Bookbinding, fine carpentry, graphology, outer space. They were hidden because no one had ever read them.

He replaced the books. The room was too hot. The sun shone directly in, and not a grain of dust moved in the shaft of light above the carpet. He felt very tired and thought that after all it might not be such a bad idea to get himself looked at, just to be on the safe side. He sat down on the sofa. Another four years, maybe five or six. Orchid cultivation seemed far-fetched. But trees, he could plant trees. Of course, that meant owning land, acquiring some acreage, buying a plot – a craving for land. Grafting, that meant breeding fruit or flowers, experimenting, getting involved in the work. Do I crave land? he thought. I don't know what I crave.

The room was far too hot. He tried to open the window but couldn't figure out how it worked and gave up.

What if I got myself a book about trees in plenty of time and tried to work up some craving? Or something else, there's so many possibilities. But maybe trees were best. And maybe he ought to know something about chemistry, as well, soil composition and the right time to plant. He was upset and he walked about the room the way a person walks about a room – over to the window, around the table, to the bedroom door, pause, back again, stopping in the middle where the sun lay on the carpet, then back to window. Finally he called a taxi. He took the valise, tossed the keys through the caretaker's letterbox on his way out. In the car he thought, I want to see how he looks. There's no need to feel sorry for him, I don't feel sorry for him, and it will be difficult to talk. But I want to see him.

There was a big tree growing on the hospital grounds, either a maple or an ash or possibly an elm. Suddenly relieved, he realised that it didn't matter in the least. If he cared about anything at all, then it was probably fruit trees.

The Storm

SHE WAS AWAKENED by a banging ventilator and lay still and listened, noticing how the storm altered the light patterns on the ceiling. The shadow of the water pipes was an unchanging cross above the head of the bed, but again and again new reflections of swaying streetlights swept across the ceiling, and sometimes the lights of cars, though there weren't many of those at this time of night. The skylight had been covered with snow for several weeks, and for several weeks he hadn't called. That meant he would never call again. Now the door to the bathroom started to bang, and she got up to close it. Without turning on the light, she walked into the front room facing the street.

The wind came in gusts and swept snow across the windows in hard, hissing blows, but it wasn't snowing. Above and beyond the storm she heard a heavy, hammering noise that she couldn't figure out. Occasionally it stopped and then resumed. Maybe roof tiles, maybe something else. The night was restless and strange, and so was the room where she listened and waited, all of it submerged in the dark, greenish radiance that surrounds a diver in the ocean. She watched as the wind-sculpted drifts on the rooftops swirled upwards like smoke. The snow and the sky above the city shared the same dark light. Something is going to happen, she thought, they've been talking about it on the radio all day. Let it come. I'm so sick and tired of being sick and tired and just waiting, and most of all I'm sick and tired of myself.

There was a light in the same two windows at the hospital, the ones always lit at four in the morning. The Christmas trees at the filling station were lit, but they were shaking their branches in the storm as if terrified and trying to tear themselves free. She stared at them for a long time, and when they finally blew down, at almost the same moment, and were swept across the street, their lights winking out, she cried out in relief. It was cold in the room, which faced the full force of the storm. It no longer came in gusts. Now the wind pressed in on the city from the sea in a single continuous roar, a rising and implacable mass of sound. Power, she thought, how I love power! The onslaught was so violent that she stepped back from the window. What a storm! What a night!

What is night? Sleeping till the next day; trying to sleep away your tiredness so you can face what you don't want to face; hiding yourself in a cautious little death for which you're not to blame – for hours that seem like seconds when you wake up. She walked back and forth between the windows and thought, Call! Call me and ask me if I'm frightened. She watched the storm tear the snowdrifts on the street into spirals and press the snow against the façades of the buildings like great outstretched hands. The greenish light had grown darker. And dreams, what are they? They dig up your fear and display it, enlarged by cruelty. There is no rest, there is no comfort!

A large object flew past her window and struck the side of the building with a crunch, then flew on – wherever, whatever. The wind was like a great groaning, a scream. Neon lights burned here and there across the city like coloured inscriptions in stone, worn almost away, and the snow rose up from the ground everywhere and from all the streets like an enormous curtain. She could no longer see any lights at all, and there was nothing she could do but listen and wait. So it goes, she thought. Thus it will be one day when everything cracks and falls and there is nothing more to remember and hold fast to, and we will have to rethink everything from top to bottom, if we have time. It won't matter if we're strong or weak, and nothing will make an impression on anyone. Everything will be erased and extinguished.

The city was empty; no people and no cars. The temperature had fallen. Her window was a whirling greenish wall of snow, and she stepped back slowly into the room. The storm had gone beyond reason and imagination, merely a powerful, uninterrupted shuddering. This shuddering was universal – in the windowpanes and the walls that protected her, in the air around her and in her teeth and her gut. She moved further back, against the wall. Right now, she thought, right now I can see that everything is utterly simple. I know what I want. Everyone is standing like this in their rooms tonight. They've woken, all of them, and don't dare go near their windows and don't dare go back to bed. They realise that it's not merely a question of living and enduring but rather of something else entirely, but they don't know what.

How can a storm of tropical strength find its way to a land of snow, a dreary, dependable land where we light Christmas trees to appease the darkness? Windowpanes shattered in well-built stone houses over the few short hours of the visitation, and sheet-metal roofs were carried away in several areas near the harbour. The storm flew into her violently opened room in an explosion of ice-cold air that was thicker than flesh. It pressed her against the wall and pressed against her eyes and eardrums and into her mouth, while all around her the room fell to pieces like the wings on a dragonfly. No truths applied and nothing had a name that could be used and recognised.

She crept towards her bedroom on hands and knees. The only thing that mattered was getting to her bed – her bed by the wall below the water pipes – and hiding in it. She felt the doorjamb with her hands. The floor was covered with snow and shards of glass, and when the storm let go of her she fell headlong and felt as if she'd broken. She crept on, reached the bed and crept in under the covers and drew them around her, tight against the wall with her knees drawn up to her chest. Now she heard the storm again and noticed she was cold and realised that something important had happened to her, something that had seemed significant and simple. But she couldn't remember what it was.

The telephone rang for a long time before she realised what it was and lifted the receiver in the dark.

"It's me," she said. "No, I wasn't asleep." She listened attentively, staring at the ceiling, which was no longer a ceiling. The window frames had become a black and arbitrary geometry. She lay beneath a grillwork of broken beams, and above them was a firmament of dark light that rose higher and higher in unbroken eddies of snow. "Don't explain," she said. "Don't say the same thing over and over again, it doesn't matter." She straightened her body in the bed. Slowly, disdainfully, she stretched out her legs and thought, It's not a bit hard to be strong. "It doesn't matter," she said again. "If you've had an insight and then lost it, don't worry about it. You'll remember it in the morning." She put her arm under her head and turned on her side. "Yes," she said. "Yes, of course I'm frightened. Do that. Call me in the morning." They said good night. She hung up the phone and fell asleep.

About seven o'clock the wind died and the snow drifted down over the city, onto streets and roofs and down over her bedroom, which was completely white and very beautiful when she awoke.

Grey Duchesse

MANDA CAME FROM A VILLAGE IN ÖSTERBOTTEN and she had second sight. It was not merely that she had prophetic dreams, she also had an unusual capacity to know when death was near and whom it intended to take. She would have preferred to keep her insights to herself, but an implacable inner voice commanded her to tell people what was going to happen. As a result, she quickly found herself shunned and eventually moved to the city where she supported herself embroidering. The whole thing was surprisingly easily arranged. Manda went to the largest ladies-wear shop, showed some work she'd done, and was hired at once. In the beginning, the job was mostly embroidering undergarments and nightdresses but later she moved on to evening gowns. Very soon she was allowed to create designs and choose colours herself, and she was given her own table behind a glass partition.

Manda seldom spoke. She didn't smile when she greeted people. That may seem unimportant, but in practice it is frightening. People are used to the smile exchanged on meeting. It is natural to smile whether you like the person or not. Moreover, she didn't look people in the eye but gazed instead at the floor in the vicinity of their feet.

Manda's silence and gravity and her undeniable skill and sense of colour – combined with the glass partition – placed her entirely in a world of her own. Those outside the partition were vaguely and uncomfortably afraid of her, but they saw no trace of arrogance or hostility in this tall, dark woman with the heavy eyebrows. When Manda came into the sewing studio in the morning, she hung up her coat and shawl (she always covered her head), and greeted the others quietly. The room always fell silent when she entered. They watched her cross the floor to her glass cubicle – a few long, hesitant steps. She moved like a long-legged animal. When she had closed the glass door, they shifted their gaze to the black shawl and coat, which was made of some cheap, wrinkled fabric and hung like an abandoned skin on its peg. No one found her clothing comic or touching, it struck them more nearly as threatening.

While Manda sat there behind her glass wall, she thought about nothing at all. She enjoyed embroidery. And Madame liked her patterns and colours very much. Manda always made a pastel sketch before beginning work. She'd carry it into the office and place it on the desk, a barely discernible outline. Madame approved it, and Manda left the office, leaving the paper behind. Patterns and colours quite naturally change as the work progresses. The sketch was a concession to the ordinary rules, nothing more, and both of them knew it.

All this time, Manda had no prophetic dreams, because she didn't know or care about the people around her. The quiet nights were a great rest and relief and made her so happy that she had no need of the days. So she just closed the glass door and embroidered. She stretched out her long, powerful legs, leaned back in her chair, and embroidered with sharp, observant eyes. Her hand plied the needle calmly, and sometimes the pretty cloth spread over her knees would rustle. It was the busy season, and the ladies came and went, but she never saw them. Nothing would have happened had it not been for the duchesse satin gown with the pearls. It was an ordinary thing in pink, an unimaginative order that Manda rescued with broad gores of grey. The lady was displeased and wanted to speak to the embroidress. Manda said she did not want to come. Madame said, "Please, Manda. It's a large order, and we can't satisfy her any other way. It's too much money."

"It's an unlucky dress," Manda said. "I don't want to come." But in the end she went.

The woman was thin and nervous, and she talked and complained without stopping. She had a bitter face and was beside herself about the grey. Manda looked at her and knew that this woman was going to die very soon and that she wasn't prepared, and at the same time she heard the inner voice that commanded her to say what she had seen. Manda felt ill. She took a long step towards the door and managed to open it. The three of them stood in a tiny fitting room and it was very hot. The woman turned and grabbed the door and shouted, "I want an explanation. I can't wear this dress the way it is!"

"You won't be wearing your dress, in any event," Manda said. Her lips were so stiff that she had difficulty talking. "You don't need this dress because you are going to die very soon." She walked back through the sewing studio and into her glass cubicle. She took her pastels and drew a new pattern as the spirit took her, with clear strong colours, mustard yellow and yellow-green, aniline blue and cobalt, orange and finally white, reckless colours that screamed loudly at first but then lay down beside one another and glowed. After a few minutes, she forgot the anxious woman who was going to die.

Madame came in and sat down. "What came over you?" she said. "Why in God's name did you say such a thing?"

"I'm very sorry," Manda answered softly. "I saw it on her and had to tell her. It was badly done."

Madame glanced at the coloured sketch. After a while, she stood up and said, with difficulty, "There must be no repetition of such behaviour."

"No. Never again," said Manda.

♦♦♦

The next day – after the woman had died in a car accident – Manda went in behind her glass partition without anyone daring to say good morning. She worked all morning and sent in her finished sketch with the errand girl and got it back approved. She began with the white evening dress and stayed and worked until the others had gone home. Then she put on her coat and shawl and went out into the city. She didn't go to her room but wandered slowly through the streets, observing everyone she met. She dared to study the faces of everyone she passed, and she could see that many of them would die very soon. Her inner voice shouted continually but the people passed quickly by. They were in a hurry, and there were more and more who were going to die, far too many, and the inner voice grew weaker and weaker. She walked on, continuing to look at everyone, and they passed her and disappeared, hour after hour. In the end, the voice went silent, and everyone looked alike.

Manda went home. She was very tired. She took up her pastels to draw a new pattern that seemed to her attractive, but suddenly she didn't know which colours to choose or why in the world they should go together in harmony.

Proposal for a Preface

SHE REMOVED THE BEDSPREAD, folded it, put it on a chair, turned on the bed lamp, and turned off the overhead. Then she opened the inner window, took out a bottle of Vichy water, closed the window, replaced the metal cap with a rubber cork, and put the bottle on her nightstand along with two sleeping tablets, her glasses, and three books. Then she drew the curtains and undressed, from the bottom up, laid her clothes on a chair and put on a nightdress and slippers. She brushed her teeth in the sink, wound the clock, saw that it said eleven o'clock, put it on the night table, turned on the radio, turned it off again, sat on the edge of the bed for ten minutes, removed her slippers, and crawled under the covers.

She put on her glasses and began reading the first chapter of the uppermost book. After four pages, she took the second book, read for a while in the middle, set it aside and opened the third book. Sometimes she read a sentence several times and sometimes she skipped a page or a couple of pages. It was very quiet, only a faint banging in the heat pipes now and then. At twelve thirty, her eyes grew tired and sleep approached, beginning in her legs. Quickly, she put her glasses and the book on the nightstand, turned off the light and turned to the wall. Immediately, and for the first time that night, she began going through everything she had said and left unsaid that day, everything she had done and not done.

She turned on the light, picked up one of the tablets, opened the bottle, swallowed the pill with Vichy water, turned off the light, and lay back down with her face to the wall.

Half an hour later, she turned on the light again, put on her glasses, opened her book, and read a chapter towards the end. She put the book and her glasses on the floor, turned out the light and pulled the covers over her head.

Twenty minutes later, she turned on the light and got up, opened the inner window, took out a packet of greaseproof paper and unwrapped the bread, sausage and cheese. She ate standing at the window. The snow lay quite deep against the windowpanes. It was snowing outside. When she had finished eating, she swallowed the other tablet with Vichy water but did not close the inner window, because the room was very warm. She lay down and turned out the light.

An hour later, she turned it on again, took off her nightdress and started walking about the room. She went to the sink, filled an enamel pitcher with water and watered her plants, took a sponge and dried the water that had run out on the windowsill and left the sponge lying by the window. She lay down and turned out the light.

About an hour later, she got up without turning on the light, turned on the radio, and turned it off again. She heard the lift, and right afterwards the newspaper came through the letterbox. She turned on the light, pulled out the top drawer of her bureau, took out stationery and a pen, and sat down on the bed. Ten minutes later, she put the paper and pen on the floor, went to the window and saw that it had stopped snowing. She turned off the light and lay down in the bed. She heard the lift again, but the heating pipes had stopped banging. Sleep drew near and her body grew heavy, sank as if with an enormous weight, and she stopped thinking and slept.

Half an hour later, she lit the lamp and looked at the clock. She got up and went to the sink and brushed her teeth. She dressed from the top down and put on water for tea. Then she looked at the clock again and realised she'd read it wrong because she hadn't been wearing her glasses. She turned off the tea water, went to the sink, filled the enamel jug, and remembered that she'd already watered the plants. It was dark outside. She put on her coat and a hat and gloves, took her purse, and stuffed her keys in her pocket. Then she opened the hall door, stepped out, closed it quietly behind her, walked down the stairs, out the door to the street, and saw it had begun to snow. She walked around the block, and when she came back to the street door she walked around the block a second time and came back and went into the building and up the stairs to begin again from the beginning.

The Wolf

THERE HAD BEEN SILENCE for far too long. She gathered herself for a comment, a polite show of interest that might save them for several more minutes. She turned to her guests and asked in English if Mr Shimomura wrote for children too. The interpreter listened earnestly, made a slight bow, which Mr Shimomura repeated. They spoke together softly, quickly, almost whispering, hardly moving their lips. She looked at their hands, which were very small with narrow, light-brown fingers – tiny, beautiful paws. She felt like a large horse.

"We are sorry," said the interpreter, also in English. "Mr Shimomura does not write. He never writes. No, no." He smiled. They both smiled. He bowed his head gently and apologetically and gazed at her steadily. His eyes were absolutely black.

"Mr Shimomura draws," the interpreter added. "Mr Shimomura would like to see some dangerous animals. Very savage, if you please."

"I understand," she said. "Animal drawings for children. But we don't have many dangerous animals. And those we have live further north."

The interpreter nodded, smiling. "Yes, yes," he said. "That is very amiable. Mr Shimomura is pleased."

"We have bears," she said uncertainly, and suddenly couldn't remember the English word for 'wolf'. "Like dogs," she went on. "Large and grey, in the north."

They looked at her attentively and waited. She tried to howl like a wolf. Her guests smiled politely and continued staring at her.

"There are no dangerous animals in the south," she repeated sullenly. "Only in the north."

"Yes, yes," the interpreter said. They were whispering again. Suddenly she said, "Snakes. We have snakes." Now she was tired. She raised her voice and said "Snake" one more time, made a creeping, wavy gesture with one hand and hissed.

Mr Shimomura was no longer smiling. He laughed, soundlessly, his head thrown back. "Anaconda," he said. "*Schlange*. Very good." Then turned off the laugh abruptly. The overweight cat jumped down from its chair and walked out into the middle of the floor.

"I," she said, with some growing panic, "I am quite old, and I don't actually know much about either children or animals."

Perhaps she could have asked or felt her way towards the world where he sought and drew his animals. Perhaps she might have discovered something new and important. It was even possible that they were looking for roughly the same thing – the dark, the wild, the shy, and the lost security of being little. She couldn't know. She lifted the coffee pot and said, "Please?"

The two of them gave a little dancing bow, rising halfway to their feet in a consummate gesture of grateful refusal.

The interpreter said, "Mr Shimomura thinks that you write beautifully. He has a present for you."

She undid the silk ribbons. Beneath several layers of brittle rice paper lay a thin wooden box that had been pieced together with the utmost precision. Inside was a fan with a painted picture of a foot-stamping warrior showing his teeth.

"How beautiful!" she said. "Tack. Thank you ever so much, you shouldn't have! I have always admired these paintings that ... And the box is exquisite ..."

"She likes the box," the interpreter said.

Mr Shimomura bowed deeply. She used the fan to fan the cat, which laid back its ears and went its way.

"Fat cat," said Mr Shimomura in his own English and laughed benevolently.

"Yes," she said. "Very fat."

The interpreter stood up and said, "This has been very interesting. Now Mr Shimomura would like to see savage animals. Please. We depend on your kindness."

♦♦♦

He opened the door for her and they walked into the chilly silence, past a row of tall brown cabinets with glass doors. A threadbare fox contemplated the ceiling from the top of one cabinet.

"Savage?" said Mr Shimomura.

"No," she said.

Mr Shimomura gazed at the fox for a long time. He was very serious. A man in a white coat came hurrying down the corridor. She stepped in his path and said, "Excuse me, but I've a foreign gentleman here who's interested in animals ..."

He stopped and looked at the floor and said, "I see. Animals. And how can I ...?"

"Dangerous native animals," she explained. "Is there any chance ...?"

"I'm in entomology," he said.

"Of course!" she said. "How silly of me. Insects are far too small."

He looked at her. "That depends," he said. "Of course, I don't know what you're after ..."

"No," she said quickly. "In this case we need something completely different." She smiled and bowed slightly and the man in the white coat continued down the corridor. Mr Shimomura had opened his sketch pad and was studying the fox with his little black eyes wide open. His profile was spare, not sculptural, only a severely drawn line, his nose hardly more than a muzzle. Only his hair spilled out in vital, almost violent profusion, like coarse, black grass. He turned to her and said, "No, no." He closed his sketchbook and waited.

They walked up the curved stairway, floor after floor, and into the uppermost hall, which was full of skeletons.

Some of them were huge and hung from the ceiling. They were equipped with black teeth and terrible, gaping jaws. Above her was the skeleton of an elephant. Without its trunk and its tusks, it had a resigned, all too human face.

"No," said Mr Shimomura.

"Yes! No!" she shouted. "I'm so sorry ..." She walked up to a glass case containing a large, bright yellow crab, put on her glasses and read aloud to hide her confusion and the silence between them. "'Japanese Giant Spider Crab, *Makrocheira kaempferi*. Normal habitat: water deep enough that wave action will not hamper its movements.' You see?" she said. "Japanese."

He smiled and bowed. They went back down the stairs. Deep, she thought. Deep enough that it doesn't feel the waves. It just walks along with its ten long legs and nothing gets in its way because it's so enormously huge.

On the next floor down they saw hundreds of animals that infinite patience and great artistry had captured in characteristic poses. They had the lassitude of death in their pelts and plaster in their jaws, but they strode across moss or sand or rock in the manner of their species, and not a single one of them was a dangerous animal.

"I'm so sorry," she said.

"Please," Mr Shimomura reassured her. For one moment his hand touched her arm. In a lovely gesture, his hands expressed the misfortune that cannot be remedied, not even with amiability. They walked on.

And then they came to the wolf.

THE WOLF

It was as moth-eaten as the fox, but it looked angrier. Mr Shimomura opened his sketchbook and she stood behind a pillar so as not to disturb him.

They were alone. The great hall was filled with an even, white light from the snow outside. There didn't seem to be any bears, only a lot of roundish seals with cotton in their eyes and, further along, in glass cases, petrified shadows with long, thin legs – probably deer. He doesn't like stuffed animals, she thought. And he's leaving tomorrow. If only my knees weren't so stiff today.

Now Mr Shimomura was standing beside her. He moved as quietly as he spoke. With a regretful gesture, he handed her his sketch pad. He had drawn the wolf with only a few lines – deliberate, brutal, tremendously sensitive lines. It was a very good drawing. Suddenly she wanted to show him a living wolf.

♦♦♦

They waited for the ferry. She had been very anxious about the silence, but Mr Shimomura didn't seem to care about her any longer. He walked around on the little strip of beach below the dock, picking up small stones and bits of charcoal and studying them closely. He must be freezing in that thin little coat, she thought. And no hat. His drawing of the wolf had given her a timid respect for him, more than what one feels for everything foreign. Her insecurity was also somewhat dampened by her concern that he wasn't warm enough.

A small motor launch with a cabin drew up to the dock. It was called the *Högholmen*.

"Doesn't the ferry run any more?" she said.

"Only the staff boat," the driver said. "And we only go three times a day."

She turned to Mr Shimomura and said, "Please." They climbed down into the motor launch.

"This man is a foreigner," the driver said. "We only take staff. It's closed in the winter."

She was suddenly upset at the thought that Mr Shimomura wouldn't get to see his wolf. "But he's leaving tomorrow. You see, he's going to Japan tomorrow and then it will be too late. This is very important to him!"

"Fine, fine," the driver said. "But I don't have any tickets." He went into the cabin.

They were the only passengers. The launch drove them out to the island, which stood tall in the water, black and white with rock and snow. She tried to remember where the cages were, but it had been a long time. She remembered a llama that had spat on her, and that she liked the monkeys because they didn't appear to be caged.

Mr Shimomura said nothing until they had gone ashore. Then he ignited his smile again, stepped aside to make space for her, and said, "Please, please." He waited for her to show him the savage animals.

She went first, up onto the island. The snow was deep and wet and there weren't many paths. They passed locked buildings and empty cages. Almost all the signs had been removed.

In the middle of the island she got her bearings. Here

was the old-fashioned pavilion with fretwork gables and an intricate pattern of very small windowpanes. It was here one drank lemonade and listened to the orchestra. Through the window she could see a sea of chairs turned upside down. The snow lay untouched on the steps. Naturally there was no place to have a cup of coffee at this time of year, and no bench to rest your legs on and nowhere to get warm. She was suddenly annoyed and turned abruptly and walked towards the birdcages where the birds sat at the tops of their trees like dark fruit. And the bears are no doubt hibernating, she thought. And it will be several hours before we can go home.

Mr Shimomura followed her footsteps in the snow. His feet were much smaller than hers. Immobile flocks of goats observed them as they walked across the island. The animals didn't turn their heads to watch them; they moved their whole bodies, all of them at the same time, with great precision, and then the forest of thick, twisted horns was absolutely motionless again. The whole area lay in silence; not a soul moved among the cages. Melting snow dropped and streamed around them. She stopped and read a sign that said, "The wild ass that came from Rostock on 5 April 1970 shares its pen with Kaisa (grey), an elderly domesticated ass". It struck her as peculiar, especially since there were no asses at all in the enclosure. She wondered where the polar bears lived.

They came down towards the shore in an area called Feline Valley. The snow leopard looked past her, uninterested. It was greyish yellow and had a very long tail. She turned around to check on Mr Shimomura, and saw that he had gone straight down to the water's edge. He was not interested in cats. She caught a glimpse of his black coat among the birch trees, moving quickly. Now he was into the yellow reeds. Maybe he's on a private errand, she thought, and looked at the snow leopard again. After a bit, she moved slowly on, stopping occasionally to wait, but Mr Shimomura did not come back. So she made her way laboriously down the bank to the shore. She didn't dare shout. The island was quiet, and maybe all the animals would started howling at once, and anyway she had no right to be there.

Mr Shimomura was walking along the water's edge, through the harbour's deposits of plastic and paper and fruit peelings. He was collecting bits of wood that the waves had washed ashore. Of course, she thought, with the relief that comes with recognition, he's collecting oddly shaped twigs. I've read that they do that.

They hadn't spoken for a long time. They were taking a break. He didn't show her his twigs, and she didn't comment. Their solitary wanderings through a closed landscape had simplified something. By and by, they walked back to the empty cages.

And now the bears came. She glanced quickly at Mr Shimomura. Yes, now he was interested. Not in the brown bears but in the polar bear. It lay on its back with its paws in the air, large and shapeless and dirty yellow against the snow. Its muzzle and eyes were coal black. It looked at Mr Shimomura over its shoulder, raised itself heavily, with the same motions as a sleepy person getting out of bed, and sat down, staring down at the snow between its paws. Mr Shimomura did not take out his sketch pad. He just looked at the bear.

The damp chill was beginning to creep up her legs. This island was really dreadful, unspeakably sad. It cut her off from everything real and alive. It scared her. Why wasn't he drawing. Was he waiting for the bear to get up? She said nothing, just tied her scarf around her head and hat and waited.

Finally Mr Shimomura turned to her, and, with a bow and a smile, let her know that now he had finished seeing the bear. They passed a bison and a mink. Behind one of the buildings there were buckets, shovels, and a pair of skis in the trampled snow. There were people who lived and worked out here. But they never saw a soul.

When she finally found the wolves, the island had darkened in the early dusk.

"Mr Shimomura," she said slowly. She smiled, almost shyly. And showed him the wolves. There were three big cages, with a wolf in each cage. All three walked back and forth along the bars, back and forth in a kind of gliding trot, without lifting their heads. Mr Shimomura went closer and gazed at them.

The wolves' ceaseless pacing struck her as appalling. It was timeless. They loped back and forth behind their bars week after week and year after year, and if they hate us, she thought, it must be a gigantic hate! She felt cold, suddenly terribly cold, and she started to cry. Her legs hurt, and she wanted to go home. The wolves and Mr Shimomura had simply nothing whatever to do with her.

It was not certain how long Mr Shimomura studied the wolves, but when he walked away the dusk had grown much deeper. She wiped her face with a glove and followed. As they passed the empty monkey house, he turned around and explained everything by laying his hand on his sketchbook, smiling, and nodding his head. He pointed to his forehead to indicate that he had captured the wolf. He had it. She needn't be the least uneasy.

They walked on up the hill. She followed after him in the resigned, irresponsible calm that follows tears, just walked through the snow and felt that now nothing more could be expected of her.

The outlook tower was locked, but there was a round, open verandah at the bottom, its walls covered with names in pencil and ink. Mr Shimomura brushed snow from the bench and sat down. He put the oddly shaped twigs beside him and sank into immobility. It was now clearly evening. The island below them was dark, but more and more lights were coming on along the half circle of the horizon, and she could hear the city's continuous dull roar and an ambulance siren that grew steadily fainter and then vanished. Maybe lions don't roar in the winter, she thought. They're sitting there somewhere in one of those windowless buildings that maintain the proper temperature. Maybe all the animals are quiet in winter if they live in cages. Her thoughts grew vague. They lingered for a moment on the Japanese giant spider crab that lives so far down on the bottom of the sea that its ten legs aren't bothered by the waves, and then she drifted into sleep.

She was awakened by Mr Shimomura touching her hand. It was time to go. She was very cold. They walked down the hill and past the pavilion. She didn't look at the cages and didn't try to say anything in English. After all, he had his wolf. One day, God knew in what remarkable place, Mr Shimomura would sit down and, with a few obvious, long-considered lines, he would draw a wolf, brutally, sensitively, the most living, breathing wolf that had ever been drawn.

The little motor launch was there to receive them. The driver said nothing.

The only thing I'd like to know, she thought, is which wolf he'll draw. The one he saw or the one he imagines.

The Rain

THREE MOTORBOATS RUSHED across the water, their bows abreast. The sun shone and the boats they met waved and assumed they were having a race.

In the middle boat, the broadest of the three, an old woman lay on a litter. The litter was made of an old red deckchair stretched out full length and supported with oars. It was narrow enough to carry through a door.

She lay with her head turned away. Her hair was very white and she seemed suddenly and surprisingly small.

The boats maintained the same speed all the way to the bus pier, where they slowed and beached at the well-trampled landing where the cars and boats of the summer people came and went and where everything was proceeding normally until the ambulance arrived. Then everyone put down their bags and baggage and thought, Dear Lord, right in the midst of vacation, and they took a grip on their children to keep them from running over to look. An old woman in a sunhat bent over and tried to look into the unfamiliar, averted face.

She wasn't being nosy, she just recognised the situation and said to herself, Poor soul.

In the general store they tried to figure out what might be needed in the ambulance and bought Vichy water, candy, and tissues.

It was hot in the ambulance. The driver knew his stuff. "Do you have any nitro?" he asked. Apparently the people who drive ambulances have to know a lot; maybe they get special training. The attendant who sat beside her just sat there, quiet and serious. He was very young and looked as if really, by natural right, he should have been somewhere else entirely. The road twisted and turned its way through the parched landscape. Once, perhaps, it had been a path, threading its way among houses and boulders and small fields. Then it grew broader, and no one stopped to think that it widened and hardened into a motor road precisely because it had always avoided obstacles.

It was a hot day and there was a thunderstorm that night. The hospital was long and low and a corridor ran through it from one end to the other. It was the darkest time of the night, but no lights were needed now in summer. All the doors stood open, and the people who lived inside them were quiet. Maybe they slept and maybe they listened to the thunder.

It was a beautiful thunderstorm. The architect who built the hospital had included a large balcony at one end of the corridor. From it, one could see the solemn garden with its asphalt paths, black with rain. A few nighttime cars drove past at long intervals. The whole landscape was filled with the storm's cold, greenish light, the trees unmoving, like painted scenery in a long and lonely stage perspective. The thunderstorm sailed over the garden, its lightning bolts white and chilly blue, losing themselves in the summer night.

The hospital was near the coast and now, just before dawn, the gulls were screaming above the shoreline. There must have been hundreds of them, all crying, the sound rising and falling, louder than the thunder. For anyone listening, their cries were like panting, like a pulse, a fervour, filling the night.

The gulls went silent when the sun rose, and the rain was brief.

The corridor was so long that it seemed to end in a point of darkness. But the whole length of the corridor glowed with the greenish light that permeated the night outside and flowed in through the open doors.

She loved thunder, but this lovely storm was probably too quiet, it never really reached her.

What is it that cuts across the breathless, brief, and occasional periods of sleep as a very tired human being dies? It cannot be merely the tormented need for more air, for water, or because everything slows and chokes as it rushes towards dissolution, towards the implacable and utterly alien transformation of the body. The old woman was visited by images, events from the life she had lived or dreamed. Everyone was with her, maybe not only those who had loved her and lived with her but also those who had slipped away, the opportunities she'd lost. There is no way to know. We know nothing but try to find explanations in a smile and a few words that come from far away, from another world, more real than reality.

Death can be a stopping, simply a going quiet. To listen to the sound of breathing for a long, long time, to laborious life fighting to continue, to life forced to continue and to run through tubes and catheters until suddenly none of them are needed and they can all be removed and hung up on their hooks and rolled away on rubber wheels. The one who dies is utterly clean, utterly silent, and then, from the grey mouth, from the altered face, comes a long cry. It is commonly called a rattle, but it is a cry, the exhausted body that has had enough of everything, enough of life and of waiting and enough of all these attempts to continue what is finished, enough of all the encouragement and the anxious fussing, all the loving awkwardness, all the determination not to show pain or frighten those you love. Death in all its variety has a million forms, but it can also be the death of a long and very weary life, a single cry, an articulation of finality, the way an illustrator completes his work with a vignette on the final page.

The thunderstorm gave the parched landscape only a quick shower.

The big rain came several days later. It started raining just before dawn, across the mainland and across the islands. Wells and water barrels filled, there was a rustling and roaring on every roof, and the rain went on and on. The soil was so dry that it was crisscrossed by cracks, and the moss came away from the granite faces in hard plates. Now all the earth, all the moss, all the roots filled with water. The rain dashed down over the whole countryside in a blessed overabundance, and inside the houses people lay listening and thought, This is good, and then turned over and fell asleep.

Blasting

NORDMAN'S BOY HAD SLOPING shoulders and large, nervous hands. His wrists were unnaturally slim. He rarely said anything – but then neither did Nordman. The trouble with the boy was that he couldn't stop working his mouth – a small, uncontrollable mouth that he tried to hide behind his hand. His eyes were much too large – astonishing, huge, Byzantine eyes in an anxious face. He tried to hide them, too, but it wasn't possible. Every time Nordman went off to do some blasting, the boy stood behind the alders and watched them load the boat. "Aren't you going to take him along sometime?" Weckström asked, but Nordman thought the boy was too little.

Now, this autumn, they had a blasting job a long way out in the islands. It was windy, and the trips home could eat up a lot of time. What with one thing and another, Nordman decided to do the whole job at once and spend the nights in the coastguard hut on Sandskär. The job could take at least two days, so he decided to take the boy with him so he wouldn't have to leave him at home alone.

They loaded their gear and got off about eight o'clock, and they ran into heavy seas once they rounded the point. The boy sat at the bow, wearing so much clothing that only his nose showed. He had never been in the motor launch before. Above him, the tarpaulin, fastened to the side rail and the cabin with big clumsy nails, had shaken out of its gussets and hung crookedly the way it always did when the wind blew from the side. A crowbar was rolling back and forth across the deck, and in the middle of the boat, black and clamouring, stood the engine, cobbled together from the parts of several other engines. It laboured there in heat and streaming oil and reeling belts, and from its innards rose a crooked metal pipe that spewed soot over the entire launch.

This machine had a dubious look to it but was actually very dependable, the product of true patience, hard mental effort, and devotion. Nordman had worked at it in the evenings almost all spring.

The seas had grown heavier, and the cardboard box at the stern had disintegrated, leaving small red apples to swim about in the bilge. The shotguns had been firmly stowed in plastic. The boy looked at everything, but all he thought about was the dynamite box, which was even better protected than the shotguns and carefully stowed away near the stern.

Nordman sat amidships, steering, and Weckström sat beside him. They passed long empty beaches, more than usually desolate because of the vacant summer cottages. Behind Herrskär they turned straight south. Then Nordman climbed across the thwarts to his son and shouted above the engine's racket, "It's fifteen tons!" He pointed south. The rock stood out no more distinctly than everything else smudged together on the horizon, but the boy nodded and understood.

"What's his name?" Weckström shouted when Nordman came back.

"Holger," Nordman bellowed.

♦♦♦

Blasting is a terrible thing to imagine, worse than anything. Someone screams, no words, just a roar, a whoop, and then boots come running, crunching across the gravel, and then a silence that is sick with dread and that grows and bulges and bursts in a great explosion. Thunder booms up out of the earth and the granite rises. Torn free by blaster Nordman, the granite rises towards the sky in dreamlike and terrible slow motion. And then it comes down. Doomsday hulks and razor-sharp splinters, shards like sharks' teeth or the jaws of saw-toothed, deep-sea monsters – they all rain down for an eternity, and you never know if, quite unnoticed, a blaster's hand is among them. In this dark image, borne by the wave of detonation, Nordman had flown into the air countless times, though he never knew.

When they arrived at Sandskär, the wind had risen to such an extent that it was just as well to spend the night and get started first thing in the morning. The island had a good harbour. There were no footprints in the sand. Holger followed the men and stood and waited while they found the key and unlocked the hut.

The cabin was very small, very dark inside, and it had an abandoned smell. There were two iron beds with water stains on the mattresses and a stove and a table with a lamp and an oilcloth. Whoever slept there last had cleaned up after themselves, but there wasn't much wood.

When they'd got the fire started, the men went after the chainsaw. After a while, he heard its high-pitched whine on the other side of the island. It screamed each time it bit off the end of a log, then it was quieter for a while and then it screamed again. A chainsaw goes through an oak plank in six seconds, and it goes through regular wood as if it were butter. When the wood breaks, it gives a jerk and the saw leaps to one side, towards the hand that holds it.

Holger didn't take off his coat and cap and didn't give a thought to the fire that was burning out. He was not an enterprising child. He rested his arms on the windowsill and looked at the waves, which were very long and wound around the island so that it was hard to tell which was the windward side and which the lea.

When his mama could still worry about Nordman, she used to sit up and wait and talk about Moses' Mountain and how wrong it was to split apart what God had joined together. It was only God's lightning that might cleave asunder, and, when the time arrived, the earth would crack and the graves would open for those who had lived a quiet life and died a natural death.

"You know what will happen," she said sadly just before she died. Nordman defended himself and said he'd never suffered from anything more serious than the flu, and then she died, and he went on blasting.

◆◆◆

He came into the hut and dropped a load of wood by the stove. He didn't look at the boy, but there was a hint of impatience in the way he fed the fire. Then he took the pail and went out again.

Nordman and Weckström could do anything. Calmly, continuously, their big boots walked in a world where they altered things and mastered them, put things together and took them apart, killed seals and long-tailed ducks and skinned them and cooked them and ate them and rarely exchanged a word. He was so scared of them, so in awe of them, that there wasn't the tiniest chance of winning their approval. It was a shame he hadn't thought to put some wood on the fire. It would have been so easy.

Now Nordman came back with the water bucket and made porridge. Weckström opened the food basket and took out the turnip loaf and some herring. "Go out and play while you're waiting," he said.

"He doesn't play," Nordman said.

After eating, the men lay down to nap. It was blowing too hard to set out a line for salmon.

◆◆◆

A fifteen-ton boulder must be enormous. When you blow it up, does it come apart in the middle like it was struck by lightning and the halves fall apart like an apple cut in two? Do the fragments fly out of a big hole, or does it split into spiny splinters, slicing knives that whirl through the air and cut off the blaster's head? What happens if Nordman is dead and his head's lying in the grass? No one will admire him any more, and no one will be afraid of him.

Holger went out and straight across the island to the launch. It was anchored a little way out, and the plastic dinghy was drawn up on the shore with the chainsaw on its side in the bow. There were clouds in the sky, and he worried about rain. Rain is bad if you're going to blast. He sat down in the sand and started digging with his hands. Pretty quickly, the hole filled with water. He tried to dig it deeper, but the sides caved in, so he stepped into it with his boots and filled in sand around them. Now he couldn't move, he was planted in the ground. He was a plant with great long roots and couldn't move or anything.

♦♦♦

The evening was fun. The lamp burned on the table and they ate sausages and potatoes and drank beer. Weckström hung a tarp over the window facing the wind, and the cabin grew warmer and warmer and smaller and smaller. But Nordman and Weckström grew large, so large that they almost reached the ceiling. After supper they did nothing, not even sleep. Their hugeness filled the room with repose and friendliness. Once, Nordman stood up and hammered a nail into the doorjamb. "That's for your coat and cap," he said, and Holger hung them on the nail himself. Pipe smoke covered the whole ceiling. When he got tired, he lay down on the bed that Nordman had made for him. The blanket smelled of motor oil. The engine was not actually as important as he'd thought. It was alone out there on the water, and, as long as it worked, no one worried about it.

Outside, the sea roared and embraced the island and the cabin and all three of them, and by and by it was deep night.

♦♦♦

At six o'clock the next morning it was still blowing, but they decided to set off anyway. It was very cold in the hut. He lay rolled up in his blanket and watched the men. The Thermos was on the table, and they drank standing up, put down their cups and started packing. Their huge shadows moved across the walls in the lamplight, back and forth.

He got dressed and took his coat and cap from the nail. Weckström took down the tarp and stood for a moment with his hands on the windowsill, looking at the weather. It was still dark, and there was no let-up in the roar of the waves.

When they stepped outside, the door blew open and banged against the wall. It was lighter outdoors, a thick grey twilight in which the men were the darkest shapes. He followed them down to the shore and stood and waited while they got the dinghy into the water.

They all climbed over into the motor launch, and he sat down on the middle seat, drew his head down between his shoulders, and waited. The engine started slowly, coughed and spluttered, and then, with a lot of heavy gasping, set itself to rights and the boat arched out of the bay. As soon as they poked their nose beyond the point, the whole grey sea swept over them, the launch rolled wildly and unpredictably, a helpless feeling until the boat and the sea got used to each other. Nordman and Weckström sat on either side of him on the middle seat, as solid as stone and smelling of wet wool. Gradually the boat began adjusting to the waves, which vaulted towards them and vanished giddily behind. Sometimes the boat stopped and shuddered from bow to stern before the screw grabbed hold again and the engine went back to work, defiantly, belts galloping. The sky above the waves had grown brighter. They were approaching the skerry with the great boulder that was a landmark from the east.

♦♦♦

He's going to blow it up. He'll light the fuse and the flames will creep along fast, and he'll stand and look at it and then turn and run! No more landmark. Heaven and earth will fly apart and, later, people will come to the skerry and step ashore and shake their heads and say, "This is where it happened."

♦♦♦

The tiny inlet was not a good spot for the boat, but they had to tie up somewhere. At least there was a cable running across it, and the stern line ought to hold. Nordman hooked a grapnel to the cable, which sank low under the weight and then went taut with each swell. "Keep an eye on it," he said to his son. "If it starts swinging, that's not good. If it flies straight up, we'll have to go back."

They took the crowbar and the box of dynamite and walked onto the skerry. Holger sat down on the granite and kept an eye on the grapnel. The launch jerked forwards with each wave and then lurched back again, pulling on the lines. The grapnel rose and dipped back down towards the water with each breaker, but it didn't swing. He watched it the whole time.

He couldn't see the boulder from down here. Will they shout or just run? How am I supposed to know when it happens?

Now Nordman started up the drill and went to work in a frenzy. The noise swallowed the wind and the waves. He held the heavy drill at an angle against the rock. He grimaced with the effort and showed his teeth. Rock dust flew about his ears, and the drill bounced and tried to find a hold, screaming in his hands. Nordman knew precisely what it could do and what it would tolerate.

Weckström sat and twisted together blasting charges.

◆◆◆

It might be that the whole thing was a huge and terrible mistake. If the world's biggest boulder sat on a skerry way out at sea, then it was probably God in his infinite benevolence who'd put it there. And then, the boy thought, then along comes Nordman. He doesn't care what God has decided. He looks at the boulder and says, This has to go!

The wind had eased. The grapnel was dipping less and less but he kept his eye on it steadily.

A little past eight o'clock, Nordman took the boy with him to the other side of the island and showed him an overhang where he could wait. "Crawl in there," he said. "And don't move. We've got another place. Do you understand?"

The boy nodded with his hand in front of his mouth. He went in under the overhang and waited.

He doesn't understand. He thinks I'm afraid. I'm not the one who gets blown up or sinks into deep, grey water. He's the one we wait for, who might never come home.

The detonation was short and muffled, a great animal growling in its sleep.

The boy shouted out loud and ran straight out onto the bare granite where he waited for the debris. And it came, fragments rained down all around him, the reality exactly like his picture of reality. There they came, saw-toothed and sliceful, heavy lumps of granite and narrow shards like spears, but they were all for him, for him and no one else. Invulnerable, he watched the fragments lay themselves to rest all around him in the order that Nordman had ordained.

Lucio's Friends

ACTUALLY, THERE'S NOTHING the matter with him except that he's so terribly nice. Maybe that's natural for a big endomorph like Lucio, but it doesn't seem to me that endless, almost heart-breaking niceness of that kind can be natural for a person who has had so many disappointments. I heard about those indirectly, not from him; he never talks about himself. I really don't believe I've ever heard him make any voluntary statement about anyone he knows or has ever known or been introduced to. It creates an empty space around him.

Of course we all love Lucio. But it's an affection that borders on despair and can even cross over into irritation.

Through his job at the Institute, he meets a great many people, and most of them consider themselves his friends after one or two encounters. That's not surprising. In every respect, Lucio meets people's expectations, no, their dearest hopes, for what they will find in a friend. Just the way he talks and listens, the way he looks at you and smiles, seems to promise an unswerving dependability.

And, believe me, one can really depend on Lucio. He is unswervingly loyal, interested, and helpful. But there are times when he completely withdraws.

Let me put that another way. The fact is that friends everywhere are constantly commenting on their other friends. With amusement, and often with love, they talk about each other's failings and peculiarities, quite simply about what their friends have said and done. A large part of all normal social life consists quite naturally of precisely this. There's no malice in it. No one would ever tell tales or make remarks in the presence of strangers that would be unthinkable. Anyway, on such occasions, Lucio withdraws. He pulls back into a kind of perplexed silence and looks down at the table. He smiles to show that his silence is not in any way reproachful. Nevertheless, you feel almost if you'd been guilty of a betrayal. And then, when the conversation turns to other topics, he lights up with such gratitude that it's almost embarrassing.

Now I don't want to paint a misleading picture of Lucio. He's not afraid of having opinions, and he defends them vehemently and happily, maybe not so much to persuade as simply to speak, to form words. His Swedish is excellent, but slow, and his choice of words is somewhat dramatic. Lucio always chooses the prettiest synonym and gives the most quotidian things a kind of melodious exaggeration, which is maybe why we don't always take him seriously. But as I said, it is only personal matters – remarks about human behaviour – that silence him. As a result, it is sometimes difficult to find things to talk about.

We see quite a lot of him, and I think we all make it clear how much we like him. I'm always amazed that he has time for so many things and yet never seems to be rushed or tired, and he always seems to have time to talk when you call him.

Every time I visit him at home, I think of chestnuts, shiny brown and white inside. I filled my pockets with them as a boy. His whole apartment is painted white, with heavy, dark-brown pieces of furniture here and there – chests and straight-backed chairs and tables that are too high and too narrow. Even Lucio's pictures are dark brown, and I could swear that he constantly polishes all of it with nut oil. We often joke about it – with great affection. Once I looked into his bedroom while he was mixing drinks in the kitchen, and, sure enough, Lucio slept in a big dark, brown bed with four tall, turned bedposts, utterly matrimonial. His eyes are the same dark, polished colour and express a disconcerted gentleness, but oddly enough he's completely bald. He ought to have long brown hair.

Lucio greets people quietly and without any kind of excess, and yet he gives everyone to believe that no meeting on earth could have given him greater pleasure. Although Lucio uses a dramatic vocabulary, we realise that it's pretty much a lexical phenomenon, so we automatically translate to what he really and truly means. And nevertheless he gives the impression that at any moment he might burst into song or throw his arms around you – in other words, go overboard. It makes us nervous and leads us to speak too openly and with larger adjectives than are really called for.

Lucio is always too cold. His apartment is full of heaters. He's bought himself a big wolfskin hat and tries to amuse us by pulling down the earflaps and growling. We laugh every time. He often does it at the wrong parties and when the parties are just starting. Lucio drinks practically nothing, perhaps a little wine with dinner. Despite his more or less natural melancholy, Lucio is a cheerful person, and he can get almost boisterous if something really amuses him. Of course we tell him funny stories (though never about sex). It's such a pleasure to watch his tense, expectant face and his boundless joy at the punch line. "That's priceless!" he cries. "How can you remember so many jokes?" Lucio never tells anecdotes himself. Come to think of it, he never tells stories of any kind but rather ruminates and comments. His intense attentiveness is less about people than about the things and day-to-day events that surround them. I'm thinking of when the conversation glides into history or antique furniture, politics, religion, or, say, deep-sea fishing or the art of gardening in the eighteenth century, whatever; then he leaps into the discussion with great enthusiasm. But he never brings up topics of that kind. He waits. Lucio reminds me of a dog, waiting alertly in concentrated, patient expectation – and then you throw the stick and the dog runs off in wild joy to bring it back.

I envy Lucio his incredible curiosity and enthusiasm, which he has managed to retain into middle age. But there are times when I'm embarrassed by his puerile amazement at what goes on in the world. He still can't get used to the fact that people travel to the moon. "Can you believe it?!" he says, lowering his voice. "They're walking around up there – on the moon! They bring home rocks!" His face is tight with astonishment and wonder. He leans forwards and touches my knee, and in a rare outburst of intimacy he tells me how he stood on Brunnspark Hill and waited, that cold winter when the Russians sent up their dog Laika into space. "I saw it pass overhead," he says quietly. "It was terribly cold, and people stood like black tombstones in the snow, one here, one there, waiting, and they all saw it. It was such a tiny light, and it moved so slowly, so high above us, arching past us in a great, long curve. It was a miracle." He opens his eyes wide and pulls in his lips and stares at me breathlessly as if he had told me some huge secret.

Or he can say, "Don't you find it touching that things start growing again every spring? New green leaves come out in the same places as before?"

Now, don't misunderstand me. Lucio isn't really naïve. He's very smart and can show real critical intelligence. Maybe it's just a question of his unusual capacity for astonishment. Sometimes when his telephone rings late in the evening and he looks at the instrument, absently and perplexedly, I could swear that he's not wondering who could be calling so late but that he's quite simply amazed at the wonderful, magical fact that a telephone can ring and convey a conversation.

It occurred to me once that we should take care of Lucio, worry about him. And, at the same time, I felt certain that none of us got as much fun out of life as he did. His childishness, if I may call it that, was completely unconscious, and as a result he wasn't able to use it to get things or avoid things, and least of all to make an impression, with the result that it was seen and accepted as charm.

It's difficult to describe Lucio now, afterwards. One thought that occurs to me is that he never talked about Italy. Why didn't he? Maybe we should have asked him about Italy.

Early on, we used to play with Italian expressions, little Italian jokes and profanities, and we'd say *Ciao* when we saw him, all of it a way of showing affection and respect. But Lucio didn't like it. He'd smile and go quiet. And sometimes there were long periods when Lucio was melancholy. He didn't turn off his phone, he welcomed us as usual, and nothing was really different except that he was sort of *playing* Lucio, if you know what I mean. He was lifeless, absent. He erected a polite façade that resembled friendliness and he tried hard in every way, but without enthusiasm. Lucio was just not Lucio.

So we left him in peace. I don't know what it was that depressed him. Sometimes I think it was the newspapers, the things happening in the world. Maybe he was homesick or missed someone who was far away. Or maybe he was just reaching the age when you suddenly look around and realise that life didn't turn out the way you'd expected. I don't know. And Lucio had so clearly and in every way shown us that he didn't want to talk about personal matters. When the mood passed, he'd start wearing his wolfskin hat again, an amusing sign that everything was back to normal.

One time I tried to cheer up Lucio by taking him cross-country skiing. We went out together and bought his equipment, and he was incredibly interested. It was a very cold Sunday, and we skied some way across the ice on the southern harbour. Of course, he wasn't doing so well, but he shuffled along behind me as best he could, straight out to where there was a boat frozen in the ice, which seemed to me a reasonable objective. When we got there, he was blue in the face and could hardly speak. "It's intoxicating," he said. "Wonderful to see. A lonely icebreaker that has itself been captured by the ice!" When we finally got home, do you know what he'd done? He had managed to fasten his bindings over his ankles, above the boot, so of course he had sores. Why couldn't he have asked or said something? But maybe he thought it was supposed to hurt.

You had to keep an eye on him constantly. He was forever making mistakes and getting cheated. Lucio's mistakes must have been gigantic back when he was courting and marrying women. Despite his reticence in such matters, it sometimes happened that I mentioned my own relationships, and he'd say, finally, very softly, "But she was so young and uncertain." Always the same thing, young and uncertain, or middle-aged and uneasy, or all the other things women can be. He always had an explanation. I know there's an explanation for everything, but insight isn't the same thing as forgiveness. And forgiveness doesn't have to mean that you forget. But Lucio forgot. He really couldn't recall the injustice and bitterness that accumulate around a life. We saw evidence of that again and again, first with suspicion but eventually with devoted relief.

Of course, we never intentionally treated him badly.

Giving Lucio presents was fun. He was always so surprised and pleased, and he showed it without your having to disparage your own gift. He never seemed to feel weighed down by gratitude, and it never occurred to him to rush out and get a present or do you some favour in return. When he did do such things, it was by chance, in passing, and he would laugh out loud if you showed you were pleased.

Now, as I try to tell you about Lucio, it's hard to understand what it was about him that we sometimes found so irritating. Not only before but especially after spending time with him, I always had a strong feeling of expectation that could last for hours. When I then try to recall what he had said, his tone of voice, his silences, his eyes, everything that had given our conversation its special character, all of it evaporated and grew unreal, like a story in a book. It was vaguely annoying. No, it was an odd feeling of helplessness – as if I'd missed or forgotten something important. It's hard to describe.

I don't know why he attached himself so exclusively to us, but I'm sure he knew that we loved him. Friendship is such a serious thing that it's hard to talk about. I've tried. But I'm afraid that I've only succeeded in explaining a fraction of the excruciating, devoted, and somewhat distant friendship between ourselves and Lucio Giovanni Marandino.

The Squirrel

ON A WINDLESS DAY IN NOVEMBER, shortly after sunrise, she saw a squirrel at the landing place. It sat motionless near the water, hardly visible in the half-light, but she knew it was a living squirrel, and she hadn't seen anything alive for a very long time. The gulls didn't count; they were always flying away. They were like the wind across the waves and the grass.

She put her coat on over her nightshirt and sat down at the window. It was cold, and in the square room with its four windows the cold stood still. The squirrel didn't move. She tried to remember everything she knew about squirrels. They sail from island to island on bits of timber, with the wind at their backs. And then the wind dies, she thought, a bit sadistically. The wind dies, or it turns, and they drift out to sea, and it doesn't turn out the way they'd imagined, not one bit. Why do squirrels go sailing? Are they curious or just hungry? Are they brave? No. Just plain stupid. She stood up and went for the binoculars. When she moved, the cold crept in under her coat. It was hard to get the binoculars focused properly, so she put them on the windowsill and went on waiting. The squirrel was still sitting on the boat beach doing nothing, just sitting. She stared at it intently. She found a comb in the pocket of her coat and combed her hair slowly while she waited.

Suddenly it ran up the granite slope, very quickly, scampered up towards the cabin and suddenly stopped. She watched the animal, intensely, critically. The squirrel sat upright, its paws hanging. Now and then its body twitched nervously, an unplanned movement, a kind of crawling hop. It scurried behind the corner of the cottage. So she went to the next window, the one to the east, then on to the south. The rock face was empty. But she knew the squirrel was still there. There were no trees and no bushes, so she'd be able to survey the island from shore to shore. She could see everything that came and everything that went. Unhurriedly, she went to the stove to start the fire.

First, two lengths of scrap timber at an angle. Above them, crisscrossed bits of kindling; between them, birch bark; finally, larger pieces of wood that would burn for a long time. When the fire got going, she started to get dressed, slowly and methodically.

She always got dressed as the sun came up, warmly and with foresight. Carefully, she buttoned her shirts and sweaters and her moleskin trousers around her broad waist, and when she'd got her boots on and pulled down her earflaps, she liked to sit down in front of the stove in unapproachable contentment, without moving, without thinking, and let the fire warm her knees. She met each new day the same way. She waited grimly for winter.

Autumn by the sea was not the autumn she had imagined. There were no storms. The island withered quietly. The grass rotted in the rain, the granite grew slippery and was covered with dark algae well above the high-water mark, and November progressed in shades of grey. Nothing had happened until the squirrel came ashore. She went to the mirror over the bureau and looked at herself. Her upper lip had a fine grillwork of small, vertical wrinkles that she hadn't noticed before. Her face was an indefinable greyish brown, like the ground outside. Squirrels also turn greyish brown in winter, but they don't lose their colour, they simply acquire a new one. She put coffee on the fire and said, "In any case, they're not artistic." The thought amused her.

Now she mustn't act hastily. The animal needed to get used to the island and above all to the cottage, needed to realise that the cottage was nothing more than an immobile grey object. But a house, a room with four windows, is not immobile. The person moving around inside stands out in sharp and threatening silhouette. How does a squirrel perceive movement in a room? How is anyone supposed to interpret movement in an empty room? The only possibility was to move very slowly, without making a sound. Living an utterly silent life was tempting, especially doing it voluntarily and not just because the island was so quiet.

On the table lay neat stacks of white paper. They always lay that way, with pencils alongside. Pages she'd written on were always turned face down. If words lie face down, they can change during the night. You see them afresh, quickly, maybe with sudden insight. It's possible.

It was possible that the squirrel would stay overnight. There was a chance it would stay over the winter.

She walked very quietly across the floor to the cupboard in the corner and opened the doors. The sea was motionless today, everything was motionless. She stood still and held the cupboard doors while she thought about what she had come to get. And as usual she had to go back to the stove in order to remember. It was the sugar. And then she remembered that it wasn't the sugar at all any longer, because sugar made her fat. These delayed recollections were depressing. She let go and allowed her thoughts to wander, and sugar led on to dogs, and she thought about what if it had been a dog that had come ashore at the landing place, but she dismissed the thought and turned if off. It was a thought that diminished the importance of the squirrel.

She started sweeping the floor, thoroughly and calmly. She liked sweeping. It was a peaceful day, a day without dialogue. There was nothing to defend or censure, everything was turned off, all the words that could have been other words or merely disowned, words that could easily have led to big changes. Now there was only a warm cottage full of morning light, full of herself, sweeping, and of the friendly noise of coffee starting to simmer. The room with its four windows was its own self-evident justification. It was safe. It was in no way the sort of place where people are closed in or left out. She drank her coffee and thought of nothing at all. She rested.

One tiny thought drifted by: What a fuss for a squirrel. There are millions of them; they're not especially interesting. One of them, one specimen, has by chance come here. I need to take care. I'm exaggerating everything at the moment; maybe I've been alone too long. But it was just a passing thought, a common-sense observation that anyone might have made. She put down her cup. Three gulls were sitting out on the point, all of them facing the same way. Now she was feeling a little sick again. It was too hot in front of the stove, and she felt ill after her morning coffee. She needed her little glass of Madeira; it was the only thing that helped.

This is the way a day begins – build the fire, get dressed, sit in front of the fire. Sweep the floor, coffee, morning Madeira, wind the clock, brush teeth, see to the boat, check sea level. Chop wood, workday Madeira. Then comes the whole day. Only at sunset do the rituals resume: sunset Madeira, lower flag, bring in chamber pot, empty slops, light lamp, supper. Then the whole evening. Every day gets written up before it gets dark, along with the water level, wind direction and temperature. List by the door jamb of what she needed from town – batteries, socks that don't itch, all sorts of vegetables, mobilat ointment, extra lamp chimney, saw blade, Madeira, shear pins.

She went to the cupboard to get her morning medicine. The Madeira was furthest in, to get the chill from the porch. She liked it cold. A bottle needs to have its appointed place. The cellar stairs under the floor were too steep and difficult, and it seemed cowardly to keep bottles hidden outside the house. There weren't many bottles left. Sherry didn't count. It made you sad and wasn't good for the stomach.

The morning light had grown stronger; there was still no wind. She ought to go in and take the bus to town to get more Madeira. Not yet but soon, before it got too cold. The motor was acting up. She ought to try and fix it, but it wasn't the spark plug this time. The only two things she understood about the motor were the spark plug and the shear pin. Sometimes she emptied out the petrol and strained it through gauze. She'd stood the motor against the wall of the cottage and slipped a plastic bag over the top. It stood there now. Of course she could row. But the boat was heavy and wanted to head into the wind. It was too far. It was all too bothersome. She turned it off.

She opened the screw top noiselessly, held the bottle between her knees and pressed the top against the flat of her hand while she twisted the bottle, coughed just as the metal band broke, poured herself a glass of Madeira with the bottle at just the right angle – and remembered that this was all unnecessary. Anyway, this was her morning Madeira, which she had a right to because she felt a little ill.

She carried the glass into the main room and put it on the table. The wine had a deep red colour against the light from the window. When the glass was empty, she hid it behind the tea canister. She went to the window and looked for the squirrel. Very quietly, she went from window to window, waiting for it to appear. She was warm from the wine, the fire burned in the stove, she turned and went anti-clockwise instead of clockwise. She was very calm. There was still no wind, and the sea merged with the sky in a grey nothingness, but the granite was black from last night's rain.

Then she saw the squirrel. It came as a reward because she was calm and had managed to turn everything off. The little animal scampered across the rock in soft, S-shaped curves, right across the island and down to the water. Now it was back at the landing place. It's going away, she thought. There's no place to live out here, nothing to eat, no other squirrels, storms come and then it's too late. Carefully, she got down on her knees and pulled the bread bin out from under the bed. Like ship's rats, animals know when it's time to leave. They swim or they sail, but one way or another they get away from what is doomed.

She crawled across the granite, moving as cautiously as she could, breaking off small bits of the hard bread and putting them in crevices in the granite. Now it had seen her and ran all the way down to the water's edge and sat motionless. She saw it only as a smudge, a silhouette, but its contours expressed alertness and distrust. Now it will leave, now it's afraid! She broke the bread as quickly as she could, faster and faster, crushing it with her fists and knees and throwing bits across the ground. She scurried into the cottage on all fours and over to the window. The landing place was empty. She waited an hour, going from window to window. The ocean was streaked with squall stripes. It was hard to see if anything out there was moving – something floating, an animal swimming. Only the birds rested on the water, white specks that then flew up and glided out over the point. The breeze marks thickened and she could see nothing at all; her eyes were tired and started to tear. She was sick of the squirrel and of herself. She was behaving like a fool.

It was time for her workday Madeira. Brushing her teeth would have to wait. So would chopping firewood and checking the sea level, all of it. She needed to watch out she didn't get too obsessive. She got her glass, filled it quickly and carelessly, and when it was empty she put it on the table and stood still and listened. The silence had changed. There was a light wind, a steady easterly breeze. The room had lost its morning light, the glow of expectation and potential. The daylight was now grey, and the new day was already used, a little soiled by mistaken thoughts and makeshift undertakings. Everything to do with the squirrel seemed unpleasant and embarrassing. She turned it off.

She stood in the middle of the room and felt the warmth of the workday Madeira and thought, This lasts only a little while. It will pass, quickly, I have to use it or renew it. All the pots and pans in a row over the stove, all the books side by side on their shelves, and on the wall her nautical instruments – those alien, decorative objects that perhaps you needed when you lived on a winter sea. But there were never any storms. If there were, she could write to someone: We're up to Beaufort eight. I'm working. The salmon floats are banging against the wall outside, and the windows are covered with foam from the waves ... No. Blinded by salt water. Fogged with ... struck blind. Spume from the breakers dashes across ... Dear Mister K. The storm has reached Beaufort eight ...

There were no storms. It just blew, nastily, stubbornly, or else there was a shiny, swollen sea that licked and nibbled at the shore. If the wind did rise, she'd have to see to the boat. When you've seen to the boat, you can have a Madeira that doesn't count.

Now the squirrel came back. A light rustling, a clattering along the cottage wall, paws scraping on the windowpane, and she saw the animal's alert little face, stupid little twitchings around its nose, eyes like glass marbles. Only for an instant, very close, and then the window was empty again. She started to laugh. Well, so you're still here, you little devil ...

Now she needed wind, any wind at all, as long as it blew from the mainland and the large islands. She tapped the barometer and tried to see if it was falling. Her glasses weren't in any of the usual places, they never were, but as usual it seemed to read 'Change'. She had to hear the weather, the weather report, and then she remembered that the batteries for the radio were dead. It didn't matter, in fact not a bit, the squirrel had stayed. She went to the list by the door jamb and wrote, 'Squirrel food'. What did they eat? Oatmeal? Macaroni? Beans? She could cook some oatmeal. They'd adapt to each other. But she wasn't going to tame it, absolutely not too tame. She would never try to get it to eat from her hand, come into the cottage, come when she called. The squirrel was not to be a pet, a responsibility, a conscience; it needed to stay wild. They would live their separate lives and just observe one another, in mutual recognition and tolerance. They would respect each other but otherwise continue doing their own thing in complete freedom and independence.

She didn't care about a dog any more. Dogs are dangerous, they react to everything immediately, they're distinctly sympathetic animals. A squirrel was better.

♦♦♦

They made ready to winter on the island. They grew accustomed to one another and developed common habits. After her morning coffee, she put bread out on the granite slope and then sat at her window and watched the squirrel eat. She had figured out that the animal couldn't see her through the windowpane and that it was probably not especially intelligent, but she still moved slowly and had grown used to sitting still for long periods, for hours, while she observed the squirrel's movements without thinking about much of anything. Sometimes she talked to the squirrel but never if it was within earshot. She wrote about it, speculations and observations, and drew parallels between the two of them. Sometimes she wrote insulting things about the squirrel, shameless accusations that she later regretted and scratched out.

The weather was unsettled and grew steadily colder. Every day, right after measuring the water level, she walked up the rock slope to the great pile of driftwood and timber scraps to chop wood. She'd select a few planks or the end of a log, then saw and chop them into firewood, diligently and rather skilfully. As she worked, she felt as strong and sure as she did sitting in front of the fire at sunrise, fully dressed, immovable as a monument, without thought. When the firewood had been chopped, she carried it down to the cottage and arranged it under the stove, carefully, each chunk, each bit of timber – triangular, square, broad, narrow, rectangles and semicircles – all tight and pretty, a jigsaw puzzle, a perfect mosaic. She had gathered the great pile of winter firewood herself.

The wind shifted constantly, and the boat lines had to be restretched and remoored. She woke up at night and lay in bed listening, worrying about the boat. She thought she heard it banging against the rock. Finally she pulled it up on land. But she woke anyway and lay in bed thinking about high water and storms. The boat needed to be pulled up higher, on trolleys. So one morning she went to the woodpile and picked out a couple of smooth old channel markers to use as rollers. She grabbed one of them and pulled. A log fell down on the far side of the pile and there was a quick, animal movement – something darted out and disappeared in headlong fear. She let go of the channel marker and stepped back. Of course it was here that it lived. It had made a nest for itself, and now the nest was destroyed. But I didn't know, she defended herself. How could I know?

She let the channel marker lie and ran back to the house for some wood shavings, ripped open the trapdoor to the cellar, remembered the torch only when she was down in the dark – she was always forgetting the torch. Jars, cartons, boxes, had she ever had wood shavings or maybe it was fibreglass she'd had, and that's not good for a squirrel, glass fibres, supposing fibreglass was in fact made of glass ... She groped around on the shelves and felt the old uncertainty, the one affecting everything that can occur in many different ways, stumbling over forgetfulness and knowledge, memory and imagination, rows and rows of boxes and you never knew which ones were empty ... I have to get a grip on myself. It's a box of cotton wadding, for the motor, a carton under the stairs. She found it and started pulling out cotton in long, reluctant tufts. The resistance and the darkness became an image of nighttime dreams, dreams about hurrying and nearly too late. She tore at the nasty, tough material and knew that she didn't have time, and then it was no longer about the squirrel but about everything, everything that can be too late. Finally she took the whole carton in her arms and tried to take it with her up the cellar stairs. It was too big. It caught in the opening. She pressed on it with her shoulders and neck, the carton burst and the wadding flew all over the floor. Now it was a question of seconds. She ran across the granite, stumbled and ran, crept round the wood pile and pushed in wadding everywhere it would be easy to find and wouldn't get wet. There you go. Build! Make yourself a nest!

Then she was done, there was nothing more she could do. Her big body had never felt so heavy. Slowly, she settled herself into a sheltered crevice on one side of the rock, drew up her legs and completely forgot the squirrel. She was safe and private, completely indifferent in her sweaters, in her boots and raincoat, deep inside a warm space of damp wool and good conscience.

♦♦♦

Shortly after noon, it started to rain. She was awakened by an insight that had ripened while she slept. It was the winter wood, the wood that was needed every day through the whole winter. Her repeated antlike trips across the granite, sawing and chopping, deeper and deeper, would make her a stubborn and merciless enemy, coming steadily closer, opening new gaps for cold and light to reach a terrified and outraged squirrel in its nest of wadding.

They'd have to divide the winter wood, that much was crystal-clear. One woodpile for the squirrel and one for herself, and it had to happen right away. Her body was stiff after her nap, but she was altogether calm because there was only one thing to be done. She went straight for the woodpile, which was as large and heavy as a house. She heaved down logs, then grabbed one end of one log and staggered with it down the rock face towards the cottage. The granite was slippery, the moss slid away beneath her boots, but she continued all the way down and tumbled the log against the wall of the cottage, then turned and walked back up the hill. They had to be carried, not rolled. A rolling log is a loose cannon, a weight crushing everything in its path.

It had to be carried, carefully, all the way to wherever it was needed. The person carrying must also be a log, heavy and unwieldy but full of strength and potential. Everything must be put in its proper place, which is what the potential is for ... I carry, steadier and steadier. I breathe a new way, my sweat is salty.

It was nearly dusk, and still raining. The trip up and down the granite slope became a quiet, automatic unreality. As she moved up and back down again, she entered a delirium of lifting and carrying and balancing, dropping the wood with a crash against the cottage wall and then walking back up. She grew strong and sure. All the words were flattened and turned off. Beams, boards, planks, logs. She tore off her sweaters and let them lie in the rain. I'm making something the way I pictured it. I'm moving what's in the wrong place and putting it in the right place. My legs strain in their boots. I could carry stones. Overturn and roll them with a crowbar and a fulcrum, huge stones, and build a wall around me with every stone in its place. But maybe there's no need to build a wall around an island.

As evening came on, she began to tire. Her legs started to wobble. She let the logs lie and carried timber instead. Finally she carried only smaller driftwood to the back wall of the cottage, while small, anxious thoughts ran through her mind. She imagined that the squirrel didn't live under the woodpile but right in the middle of it, where it wasn't damp. She'd made a mistake. Every time she raised a plank, it was maybe that particular plank that formed the roof of the squirrel's nest.

Every piece of wood she lifted could disturb or destroy. Whoever dared touch this woodpile must calculate exactly how the logs lay and how they balanced one another, must think calmly and wisely and precisely, know when to heave on a log and when to tease it out with care and patience.

She listened to the whispering silence over the island, to the rain and the night. It's impossible, she thought. I won't go up there again. She returned to the cottage and undressed and went to bed. She didn't light the lamp this evening, which was a violation of ritual, but it would show the squirrel how little she cared about what happened on this island.

♦♦♦

The next morning, the squirrel did not come to eat. She waited for a long time, but it didn't come. There was no reason for the squirrel to feel hurt or suspicious. Everything she had done was simple, unambiguous, and fair. She had divided the woodpile and withdrawn. More than fair. The squirrel's woodpile was several times larger than her own. If the animal had the least personal trust in her, if it perceived her in any way as a friendly fellow creature, then it must see that from the very beginning she had tried to help.

She sat down at the table. She sharpened her pencil and put a sheet of paper on the desk in front of her, perpendicular, parallel with the edge of the table. This always made the squirrel easier to understand.

If now, in spite of everything, the squirrel saw her as movement, as an object, something unimportant and insignificant, then that also meant it did not see her as an enemy. She tried to concentrate. She made a serious effort to imagine how the squirrel perceived her and in what way its fright at the woodpile might have changed its attitude. It was possible that the squirrel had been nearly ready to begin liking her and was then seized by distrust at that decisive moment. On the other hand, if it regarded her as nothing special, as a part of the island, a part of everything that withered as autumn swept on towards winter, then it would not see the episode at the woodpile as a hostile gesture but rather as a kind of storm, the kind of change that ...

She was suddenly tired and started drawing squares and triangles on the paper. The squirrel seemed harder and harder to understand. She drew serpentine lines between the squares and the triangles and tiny little leaves growing out in every direction. The rain had stopped. The sea was swollen, shiny and tumid – such eternal chatter about the beauty of the sea! And then she saw the boat.

It was a long way off, but it was coming, it was moving. It had an inorganic shape that was neither gull nor stone nor buoy. The boat was coming straight towards the island. There was nothing out here to head for except the island. Boats in profile are harmless. They pass along the marked channels, but this one was headed straight on, black as a flyspeck.

She grabbed up her papers – several fluttered to the floor – and tried to push them into the drawer, but they bunched up and refused to go in. Anyway, it was wrong, quite wrong, they should lie out in plain sight, where they'd be discouraging and protective. She pulled them out again and smoothed them. Who was it who came, who dared to come? It was them, the others; now they'd found her. She ran around the room moving chairs and objects, then moving them back again because the room was unalterable. The black dot had come closer. She grabbed the edge of the table with both hands, stood still and listened for the sound of the motor. There was nothing she could do. They were coming. Coming straight at her.

When the sound of the motor was very close, she threw open the window on the back side of the cottage, jumped out, and ran. It was too late to launch her own boat. She bent over, ran to the far side of the island and slipped down into a crack in the granite near the shore. From here, she could no longer hear the motor, only the slow motion of the waves on the rock. What if they came ashore? They see the boat. The cottage is empty. They start to wonder, they walk up onto the island, and they see me crouching here. It won't do. I have to go back. She started to crawl, slowing down as she approached the top of the island. The motor had stopped. They'd gone ashore. She lay down full length in the wet grass, inched herself forwards a couple of metres and rose up on her elbows to have a look.

The boat had anchored over a bank not far from the island. They were fishing. Three square-shaped men sat beside their rods, drinking coffee from a Thermos. Possibly they were talking a bit. Occasionally they reeled in their lines. Maybe they had caught some fish.

Her neck got tired and she let her head sink onto her arms. She didn't care about squirrels, not about the men fishing, nor about anyone; she just slid down into a great disappointment and admitted to herself that she was disappointed. She thought, How can this be? Why am I beside myself because they're coming and then terrifically disappointed when they don't come ashore?

The next day, she decided not to get up at all. It was a melancholy and defiant decision. She thought no further than this: I will never again get up. It was a day with rain, a quiet, steady rain that might continue for days. That's good, I like rain. Curtains and draperies of rain, endless infinities of rain going on and on, pattering – rustling and pattering – across the roof. Not like sunshine, which hour by hour moves through the room like a challenge, crossing the windowsill, the rug, marking the afternoon on the rocking chair, then disappearing on the stove hood in red, like an accusation. Today is honourably and simply grey, an anonymous, timeless day that doesn't count.

She made a warm cavity for her heavy body and drew the covers over her head. Through a little air hole for her nose she could see two pink wallpaper roses. Nothing could get at her. Slowly she drifted back to sleep. She had learned to sleep more and more. She loved sleep.

♦♦♦

The rain darkened towards evening, when she woke up hungry. It was very cold in the room. She wrapped herself in her blanket and went down to the cellar to get a tin of food. She forgot the torch and took a tin at random in the dark. And stopped, listening, stock-still with the tin in her hand. The squirrel was somewhere in the cellar. There was a tiny scurrying sound and then silence. But she knew it was there. It was going to live all winter in her cellar, and its nest could be anywhere. She'd have to leave the vent open and make sure it didn't get covered with snow. And she'd have to move all the tinned food and everything else she needed up into the cottage. And, nevertheless, she'd never know for sure if the squirrel was living in the cellar or the woodpile.

She went up and closed the trapdoor. The tin she'd brought with her was boiled mutton with dill sauce, which she didn't like. A belt of clear sky had opened up at the horizon, a narrow, glowing band of sunset. The islands lay like coal-black streaks and lumps in the burning sea. The fire burned all the way to the shore, where the waves swallowed it and then slid around the point in the same curve over and over again as they broke over the slimy November granite. She ate slowly and saw how the red deepened across the sky and the water, a violent, unthinkable crimson. And then suddenly the red winked out, everything went violet, lapsed slowly to grey and then into early night.

She was wide awake. She dressed and lit the lamp and all the candles she could find, got a fire going in the stove. She turned on her torch and put it in the window. Finally she hung a paper lantern outside the door, where it shone clearly and steadily in the quiet night. Now she took out the last of the Madeira and put it on the table beside her glass. She walked out onto the rock and left the door open. The glowing cottage was beautiful and mysterious, like a lighted porthole in a foreign ship. She walked all the way to the end of the point and began walking around the island, very slowly, right at the water's edge, and the whole time she turned her face towards the wide-open darkness of the sea. Only when she'd walked around the entire island and had come back to the point would she turn and consider her illuminated cottage. Then she'd walk straight into its warmth, close the door, and be home.

♦♦♦

When she came into the cottage, the squirrel was sitting on the table. The animal dashed away, the bottle fell and started to roll, she leaped forward too late, and the bottle shattered on the floor. She got shards of glass between her fingers, and the rug soaked up a dark Madeira stain.

She raised her head and looked at the squirrel. It hung on the wall among the books, legs outspread, heraldic, immobile. She stood up and took one step towards the squirrel; one more step; it didn't move, and she stretched out her hand towards the animal, closer and closer, very slowly – and the squirrel bit her, quick as lightning, sharp as scissors. She screamed and went on screaming with rage in the empty room. She stumbled across the broken bottle and outdoors, where she stood and bellowed at the squirrel. Never ever had anyone forfeited a confidence, misused a covenant the way this squirrel had done. She didn't know if she had reached out her hand to the animal in order to caress or strangle it. It didn't matter; she had reached out her hand. She went in and swept up the broken glass, blew out all the candles and put more wood in the stove. Then she burned everything she had written about the squirrel.

♦♦♦

In the time that followed, none of their rituals changed. She put out food on the rock slope and the squirrel came and ate. She didn't know where it lived and didn't care. She no longer went into the cellar or up to the woodpile on the hill. It showed her contempt, an indifference that didn't stoop to revenge. But she moved about the island differently, impulsively. She could rush out of the cottage and slam the door behind her. She rattled the pans and stomped on the floor. Finally she started running. She would stand still for a long time, motionless, and then set off across the granite, running and panting back and forth across the island, flapping her arms and screaming. She didn't care in the least whether the squirrel saw her or not.

One morning it had snowed, a thin covering of snow that didn't melt. Now the cold was coming. She must get the motor running, go to town, buy things. She went and looked at the motor, picked it up for a moment and then put it back against the wall of the cottage. Maybe in a few days. The wind was blowing. Instead, she started looking for the squirrel's paw prints in the snow. The ground was white and untouched around the cellar airhole and the woodpile. She walked the shoreline, walked the whole island systematically, but the only prints she found were her own. Clear and black, they cut the island into rectangles and triangles and long curves.

Later that day, she grew suspicious and looked under the furniture in the cottage, opened drawers and the cupboard. Finally she climbed up on the roof and looked down the chimney. You little bastard, you're making me ridiculous, she said to the squirrel. Then she went to the point and counted the pieces of timber, the squirrel boats she'd set out for a following wind to the mainland in order to show the squirrel how little she cared for it. They were still there, all six. For a moment she was uncertain. Had there been six, or maybe seven? She should have written it down. Not writing it down was indefensible. She went back to the cottage, shook out the rug and swept the floor. Nowadays everything got out of order. Sometimes she brushed her teeth in the evening and didn't bother to light the lamp. The lack of order was because she no longer had the Madeira to divide the day into proper periods and make them clear and easy.

She washed every window and rearranged the bookcase, not by author this time but in alphabetical order by title. When she'd finished, she happened to think of a better and more personal system and decided to arrange the books according to herself – the ones she liked most on the top shelf; the ones she liked least on the bottom. She discovered to her amazement that there wasn't a single book she liked. So she let them stay the way they were and sat down by the window to wait for more snow. There was a bank of clouds to the south. They might bring snow.

♦♦♦

That evening she felt a sudden wish for company and went to the top of the island with her walkie-talkie. She pulled up the aerial, turned it on, and listened. There was a distant scratching and swishing. A couple of times she'd picked up conversations between two boats. It might happen again. She waited for a long time. The night was coal-black and very quiet. She closed her eyes and waited patiently. She heard something very far away, no words but two voices talking to each other. They were slow and calm. They came closer, but she couldn't make out what they were saying. She heard that they were winding up their conversation, their tone of voice changed and their sentences got shorter. They were saying goodbye, and it was too late – and she started screaming, Hello, it's me, can you hear me, although she knew they couldn't, and then there was only the distant swishing noise and she turned it off. Stupid, she said to herself. It occurred to her that the walkie-talkie batteries might work in the radio and she went back to have a try. They were the wrong size. She needed to go into town. Madeira, batteries. Under 'batteries' she wrote 'nuts' and then crossed it out. It was gone. There must have been seven pieces of wood after all, and not six, all at precisely the same distance from the water, sixty-five centimetres.

She read through her list and suddenly it was an inventory in a foreign language and seemed completely alien. Shear pins, mobilat ointment, powdered milk, batteries, a catalogue of strange, unreal items. The only thing that mattered was the bits of timber, whether there'd been six or seven. She took her measuring tape and torch and went down to the shore again. The shore was barren, completely clean. There were no pieces of timber at all, not one. The sea had risen and taken them.

She was utterly amazed. She stood at the shoreline and shone her torch down into the water. The beam broke the surface and lit up a grey-green watery cavern that grew darker as it went down and was filled with very small, indistinct particles that she had never noticed before. She shone the beam further out over the water and into the darkness. And there the weak cone of light captured colour, a clear yellow colour, a varnished wooden boat drifting away on the breeze.

She did not understand right away that it was her own boat. She just stared at it, noticing for the first time the helpless, dramatic bobbing of a drifting boat, an empty boat. And then she saw that the boat wasn't empty. The squirrel sat on the rear thwart, staring blindly straight into the light. It looked like a piece of cardboard, a dead toy.

She made half a movement to take off her boots but stopped. The torch lay on the rock and was shining at an angle down through the water, a rampart of swollen seaweed that swayed as the sea level rose, then darkness where the rock curved downwards. The boat was too far out. It was too cold. It was too late. She took a careless step and the torch slid into the water. It did not go out; it stayed on as it sank along the side of the rock face, a smaller and smaller vanishing light that illuminated quick glimpses of a ghostly brown landscape with moving shadows, and then there was nothing but darkness.

"You damned squirrel, you," she said slowly and with admiration. She stood there in the darkness in continuing astonishment, a little weak in the legs and vaguely aware that now everything was radically altered.

Eventually she found her way back across the island. It took a long time. It was only when she closed the door behind her that she felt relief, a great, elated relief. All decisions had been taken from her. She no longer needed to hate the squirrel or worry about it. She didn't need to write about the squirrel, didn't need to write about anything at all. Everything was decided, everything solved, with a clear and unconditional simplicity.

It had begun to snow outside. It snowed thick and quiet. Winter had come. She put more wood on the fire and turned up the lamp. She sat down at the kitchen table and started to write, very rapidly.

On a windless day in November, shortly after sunrise, she saw a person at the landing place.

Also by Tove Jansson

THE SUMMER BOOK

"*The Summer Book* is a marvellously uplifting read, full of gentle humour and wisdom." Justine Picardie, *Daily Telegraph*

An elderly artist and her six-year-old granddaughter while away a summer together on a tiny island in the Gulf of Finland. As the two learn to adjust to each other's fears, whims and yearnings, a fierce yet understated love emerges – one that encompasses not only the summer inhabitants but the very island itself. Written in a clear, unsentimental style, full of brusque humour, and wisdom, *The Summer Book* is a profoundly life-affirming story. Tove Jansson captured much of her own life and spirit in the book, which was her favourite of her adult novels. This edition has a foreword by Esther Freud.

A WINTER BOOK

"As smooth and odd and beautiful as sea-worn driftwood, as full of light and air as the Nordic summer. We are lucky to have these stories collected at last." Philip Pullman

A Winter Book features thirteen stories from Tove Jansson's first book for adults, *The Sculptor's Daughter* (1968), along with seven of her most cherished later stories (from 1971 to 1996). Drawn from youth and older age, this selection by Ali Smith provides a thrilling showcase of the great Finnish writer's prose, scattered with insights and home truths. It is introduced by Ali Smith, and there are afterwords by Philip Pullman, Esther Freud and Frank Cottrell Boyce.

FAIR PLAY

"So what can happen when Tove Jansson turns her attention to her own favourite subjects, love and work, in the form of this novel about two women, lifelong partners and friends? Expect something philosophically calm – and discreetly radical. At first sight it looks autobiographical. Like everything Jansson wrote, it's much more than it seems ... *Fair Play* is very fine art." From Ali Smith's introduction

What mattered most to Tove Jansson, she explained in her eighties, was work and love, a sentiment she echoes in this tender and original novel. *Fair Play* portrays a love between two older women, a writer and artist, as they work side by side in their Helsinki studios, travel together and share summers on a remote island. In the generosity and respect they show each other and the many small shifts they make to accommodate each other's creativity, we are shown a relationship both heartening and truly progressive.

THE TRUE DECEIVER

"I loved this book. It's cool in both senses of the word, understated yet exciting ... the characters still haunt me." Ruth Rendell

In the deep winter snows of a Swedish hamlet, a strange young woman fakes a break-in at the house of an elderly artist in order to persuade her that she needs companionship. But what does she hope to gain by doing this? And who ultimately is deceiving whom? In this portrayal of two women encircling each other with truth and lies, nothing can be taken for granted. By the time the snow thaws, both their lives will have changed irrevocably.

TRAVELLING LIGHT

"Jansson's prose is wondrous: it is clean, deliberate; an aesthetic so certain of itself it's breathtaking." Kirsty Gunn, *Daily Telegraph*

Travelling Light takes us into new Tove Jansson territory. A professor arrives in a beautiful Spanish village only to find that her host has left and she must cope with fractious neighbours alone; a holiday on a Finnish island is thrown into disarray by an oddly intrusive child; an artist returns from abroad to discover that her past has been eerily usurped. With the deceptively light prose that is her hallmark, Tove Jansson reveals to us the precariousness of a journey – the unease we feel at being placed outside of our millieu, the restlessness and shadows that intrude upon a summer.

ART IN NATURE

An elderly caretaker at a large outdoor exhibition, called Art in Nature, finds that a couple have lingered on to bicker about the value of a picture; he has a surprising suggestion that will resolve both their row and his own ambivalence about the art market. A draughtsman's obsession with drawing locomotives provides a dark twist to a love story. A cartoonist takes over the work of a colleague who has suffered a nervous breakdown only to discover that his own sanity is in danger. In these witty, sharp, often disquieting stories, Tove Jansson reveals the faultlines in our relationship with art, both as artists and as consumers. Obsession, ambition, and the discouragement of critics are all brought into focus in these wise and cautionary tales.